An Unnatural Death

"Earth to earth, dust to dust." Reginald made a face of humorous disgust and looked round to see whether his friends were appreciating it. "Bit grisly, isn't it? Don't feel at all dusty myself—not just yet."

"Where's Clive?" asked one of the black-clad ladies, stopping suddenly.

The others paused too, and most of them turned to look back at the grave. The dark young man was still standing on its brink, and even at this distance his excessive agitation was noticeable. He was kicking little bits of earth forward on to the coffin, and shaking his head furiously from side to side.

"Excuse me," said the vicar, detaching himself from the group and hurrying towards the grave. "Clive, Clive," he said gently, "you must come away now."

Clive raised a white face and stared at the vicar. Not only did he look seriously shocked; he also looked scarcely sane.

"He killed her," cried Clive in a loud voice. "He killed my mother!"

ANNA CLARKE

LETTER FROM THE DEAD

CHARTER BOOKS, NEW YORK

This Charter book contains the complete
text of the original hardcover edition.
It has been completely reset in a typeface
designed for easy reading, and was printed
from new film.

LETTER FROM THE DEAD

A Charter Book / published by arrangement with
Doubleday, a division of Bantam, Doubleday,
Dell Publishing Group, Inc.

PRINTING HISTORY
Doubleday edition published 1981
Charter edition / January 1989

ISBN: 1-55773-147-0

Charter Books are published by The Berkley Publishing Group,
200 Madison Avenue, New York, New York 10016.
The name "CHARTER" and the "C" logo
are trademarks belonging to Charter Communications, Inc.

PRINTED IN THE UNITED STATES OF AMERICA

10 9 8 7 6 5 4 3 2 1

1

"We therefore commit her body to the ground; earth to earth, ashes to ashes, dust to dust . . ."

The Reverend Nevil Grey, vicar of St. Mark's Church in Southdene, Sussex, stifled a cough before he spoke the words that had been heard beside so many newly-dug graves throughout the centuries.

Though it is nearly always cremation nowadays, he thought, and even while he prayed silently and sincerely for both the living and the dead, he was shiveringly aware that the chapel at the crematorium was much warmer than the churchyard on this raw February morning, and hoped that he was not in for a bout of bronchitis. His daughter Angela had wanted him to get someone else to take the service, and had even suggested that they should summon the curate back from his week's holiday, but Nevil had insisted on coming himself.

Maureen Myrtle, third wife of the celebrated novelist Reginald Myrtle who had bought the Old Manor some years ago, had clung to Nevil's hand when he visited her in her illness and begged him never to desert her and never to let her be taken away from Southdene, alive or dead. She had been born and brought up in the old village, in the days before Southdene had been extended into a thriving industrial community; the village green, the duckpond, and above all, the Norman church with its surrounding yews and ancient elm trees backed by the gentle rise of the South Downs, held happy memories for her, to which she had returned more and more during the last painful and frightened weeks of her life.

"Almighty God, with whom do live the spirits of them that depart . . ."

Nevil Grey glanced round at the little group of mourners standing in the shelter of the yew hedge at this far corner of the churchyard where the snowdrops grew. The bereaved husband, in dark coat and holding a fur hat, shifted restlessly from one foot to the other and glanced at the vicar from time to time with an uneasy look in his eye. Not from grief, surely, for it was common knowledge that the lady who would no doubt become the fourth Mrs. Myrtle was already settled in the house; but it might be that listening to the words of the funeral service had aroused in Reginald one of his occasional attacks of guilt and superstitious fear.

The young woman in jeans and heavy sweater standing next to him, his daughter by a former marriage, seemed unaffected by the reminder of the littleness of mortal man in the face of eternity, for she was openly yawning; and a casually dressed middle-aged couple, friends of the widower, were listening with courtesy and respect, but were obviously not the least bit emotionally involved in the proceedings.

Beyond them four more middle-aged people huddled together. They were all dressed in dark clothes and looked awkward and cold, but not entirely indifferent. Brother and sister of the dead woman, with their respective spouses; not very close to her, not very keen to leave their homes and their own affairs and make a long journey in this unfriendly weather, but nevertheless genuinely moved in their various ways by her death.

And beyond them again, at a little distance from the rest

of the mourners, stood a young man in his early twenties with his dark head bowed and his hands thrust deep into the pockets of his green anorak. He appeared quite calm, but the vicar had been anxiously conscious of his demeanour throughout the proceedings. This was Clive Bradley, illegitimate son of the dead woman and probably the only one present who was truly mourning her loss. He was tall and well-built, and would have been good-looking had it not been for the brooding, almost sullen expression on his face. But then how could he look otherwise, thought Nevil; he's not only lost his mother, he's lost the only place he could call his home. For there was no love lost between Clive and his stepfather. The Vicar himself had been the witness of several minor explosions of temper during his visits to the house and he had no doubt that many others, far worse, had taken place when there were no strangers present.

"Please don't desert Clive," the dying woman had begged. "He's going to need help so badly."

And so Nevil had added this promise to the others that he had made her.

". . . be with us all evermore. Amen."

The vicar ceased speaking and allowed himself the relief of a cough. Earth was thrown on the coffin. The group of mourners moved thankfully off the wet grass and on to the gravel path and Reginald Myrtle came towards Nevil with outstretched hand and a faint smile on his handsome but somewhat too fleshy face. Eats and drinks too much, thought the vicar; he'll be having another heart attack and sending for me in a panic to make his confession; I don't think I can stand that again—I'll have to send Ronnie.

Thank you, Vicar," said Reginald with affable condescension. "Beautiful language, isn't it, the funeral service? And beautifully spoken, if I may take the liberty of saying so. But then of course you believe it all, don't you? That's your job."

He dislikes me as much as I dislike him, thought Nevil; we'd better keep apart as much as possible when this is over. Aloud he said politely: "It is not common to use this form of the service nowadays, but that was Mrs. Myrtle's wish."

"Earth to earth, dust to dust." Reginald made a face of humorous disgust and looked round to see whether his friends were appreciating it. "Bit grisly, isn't it? Don't feel all that dusty myself—not just yet."

His daughter made a grimace of sympathy, but the middle-aged couple did not react, and Mrs. Myrtle's relatives looked positively disapproving as the whole group moved towards the lych-gate.

"Where's Clive?" asked one of the black-clad ladies, stopping suddenly.

The others paused too, and most of them turned to look back at the grave. The dark young man in the green anorak was still standing on its brink, and even at this distance his excessive agitation was noticeable. He was kicking little bits of earth forward on to the coffin, and shaking his head furiously from side to side.

"Excuse me," said the vicar, detaching himself from the group and hurrying towards the grave. "Clive. Clive," he said gently, "you must come away now."

The young man said nothing. Nevil could see him trembling.

"If you can't face going back with the others, would you like to come and sit with Angela and myself for a little while?" suggested Nevil.

Clive raised a white face and stared at the vicar. Not only did he look seriously shocked; he also looked scarcely sane.

"He killed her," cried Clive in a loud voice. "He killed my mother!"

"No, Clive. She died of cancer. It came on quite suddenly, but it was blessedly short."

"He killed her, he killed her!" repeated Clive, taking no notice of the vicar, his voice becoming more and more hysterical.

Nevil looked anxiously towards the group of people now

standing under the lych-gate. They appeared to be talking to each other, but he felt sure that they had all heard Clive's words and were very deliberately not looking in his direction. Emotional scenes by the graveside are seldom seen now, he thought; just as well, since nobody knows how to deal with them. Open grief is unforgiveable. Nevil's heart went out to the young man so recently bereaved and so ill-prepared to cope with it. He longed to offer consolation but was fearful of how it might be received.

"Will you do something for me?" he asked.

The wild-looking eyes appeared to come into focus, and Nevil believed that he was being listened to.

"Would you mind going over to the vicarage and letting Angela know that I'll be a little later than I said? I promised to be home by twelve-thirty but it's past that now and there are still a few things to attend to. It will be quicker if you go out here by the side gate." For a moment it looked as if the ruse to keep Clive away from his stepfather had succeeded. Clive muttered something inaudible, turned his back on the grave, and took a few steps in the direction of the little wicket-gate that led straight into the vicarage garden.

"Thanks," called Nevil after him. "I shan't be long."

And he hastened back to the group at the lych-gate, determined to hustle them all into their cars as quickly as possible.

"Is that the lot then, Vicar?" said Reginald. "Nothing more to be done here? Then off we go to the booze and the bean-feast. Nonsense, man," he said to his brother-in-law who was protesting that they would rather go straight home. "Of course you must stay and take a bite. It's customary at funerals. Where's that boy? Most inconsiderate to keep us hanging about like this. He can moon over his mother's grave for ever after if he likes, but he ought to come and do his stuff now. Clive! Clive!"

Reginald Myrtle's voice was very carrying. It had filled many a lecture hall and talked down many a colleague on a brains trust or at a committee meeting. Clive, who had been walking across the rough patch of grass where the snow-drops grew, had just reached the little wicket-gate.

Oh go on, go on, prayed the vicar silently: take no notice of him, he's doing it on purpose to provoke you. But the damage was done, and nothing short of brute force could prevent the confrontation now. Or an accident, perhaps. If somebody were to faint . . .

The Reverend Nevil Grey was suddenly seized with a violent fit of coughing. It was partly a genuine fit, aggra-vated by cold and nervous strain, but he was not without hope that it would distract everybody's attention. Maureen Myrtle's relatives did, in fact, express their concern and start producing cough sweets from their pockets and hand-bags, but Reginald continued to stare at Clive, who came rushing straight across the churchyard, jumping over graves, brushing against tombstones, and even knocking over a pot of flowers. When he reached the lych-gate he was panting and there was the half-crazy look in his eye that had alarmed the vicar earlier. He raised his arms and clung to one of the sloping wooden beams and stood there swaying and glaring at Reginald.

"Clive," ventured his mother's sister, "don't you think you had better come home now and rest a little. After all this strain . . ."

Her feeble attempt to defuse the tension only made matters worse. Clive let go of the beam and rounded on her.

"Home!" he cried bitterly. "You call that place home! You've no idea what it's been like. You just kept away, didn't you, Aunt Sarah? You didn't want to know what Mother was going through."

"Well really, Clive," began Aunt Sarah in an offended voice.

"I don't think you ought to talk to your aunt like that," interposed her husband. "She's not been at all well lately and if I'd had my way she wouldn't be here today."

"Oh no, Geoffrey. I had to come and see Maureen laid to

rest. And after all, Derek and Evelyn had even further to come."

"Very inconvenient, having to leave the business for a couple of days just now," said Maureen Myrtle's brother Derek.

The vicar noticed that Reginald and his friends had been exchanging amused glances during this conversation, and for a moment or two he had hopes that the threatened row between Clive and his stepfather might be swallowed up in general family bickering.

"It was very good of you all to come," he said firmly, "and I am only sorry that you have had the discomfort of a burial on such a cold day. It was, as you all know, Mrs. Myrtle's own wish to be buried here in this churchyard and not to be cremated or taken to the municipal cemetery. Shall we move on out of the cold now?"

There was a murmur of assent and a shuffling movement from all the group except Reginald and Clive.

"Are you coming, Clive?" asked his Uncle Derek, looking back towards the lych-gate, and at the same time Reginald's daughter Jill called out impatiently: "Oh do hurry up, Dad! I'm absolutely frozen."

But her father took no notice. He was standing quite still with his hands in the pockets of his overcoat, staring at Clive. He was not a tall man, and even his fur hat and the built-up platform shoes that he wore did not bring his height up to that of the boy. Clive was hugging himself, his bare hands showing blotched with the cold as they gripped the sleeves of his anorak. For warmth? Or to stop himself from hitting his stepfather, thought the vicar as he replied politely to a question from Clive's Aunt Sarah.

"No, I will not be joining you for lunch. My daughter is waiting . . ."

But Sarah Delaney was no longer listening to him. She and all the rest of the group were completely gripped by the little drama that was taking place under the gable of the lych-gate. Clive, still hugging himself, was thrusting his face forward threateningly towards Reginald.

"And you know why she wanted to be buried and not cremated!" he was shouting. "It's so that she could be exhumed and a post-mortem held. You thought you'd get away with it, didn't you? Bribing the doctor and having your girl-friend to nurse her. But just you wait. Just you wait. I'll get my evidence and when I get it and they dig her up and find out just what you did—"

"I think you had better try to control yourself." Reginald's voice cut coldly and clearly into the young man's tirade.

"—you and your girl-friend," continued Clive, taking no notice of the interruption. "Having her before my mother was even dead!" His voice trembled more than ever as he went on. "Why did you have to kill Mother? Why couldn't you just leave her? She wouldn't have tried to stop you. You didn't have to kill her."

The voice shook so much that he sounded as if he were about to cry.

"I have to remind you," said Reginald icily, "that there is a law of slander and we have a number of witnesses within earshot."

"I don't care!" shouted Clive, raising his head and looking about him wildly. "I want them to hear. I want everyone to know what you've done."

"Very well then. If you continue in this manner I shall either sue you for slander or have you certified as insane. One or the other. Take your choice."

Reginald swung round on his heel and came towards the mourners.

"I must apologize for that little incident," he said smoothly. "We have had rather a lot of this sort of thing these last weeks, as our reverend friend here can testify." And he glanced in his patronizing manner at Nevil, who beneath a deadpan exterior was feeling increasingly sympathetic towards Clive. "I was afraid we wouldn't get through the funeral without an outburst," continued Reginald, "but I hope that will be all for the present. I have been conferring with Dr. Jephcott—our excellent GP here who also happens to be a fellow-author though under a pseudonym of course—and he has recommended a psychiatrist who has been very successful with cases of hysterical paranoia in young people. The difficulty, of course, will be to persuade Clive to go for treatment, but I shall do my best."

He shepherded the group towards the cars.

"If you people," he continued, turning to his deceased wife's relatives, "could perhaps put in a timely word with Clive . . ."

The Reverend Nevil Grey could trust himself to listen to Reginald Myrtle no longer. That man is capable of anything, he muttered to himself as he hurried back through the churchyard; even of murder, but no sense in having a row with him now—must see to that poor boy.

Clive had returned to his mother's grave and was clinging to a neighbouring tombstone and shaking with sobs. The vicar took him by the arm.

"Come on now," he said. "This isn't helping you and it certainly isn't helping my cough. And I'm going to get scolded by Angela but I dare say she'll manage to make the lunch stretch to three. Come on now, Clive. Let's go and get warm."

And with only a token show of resistance Clive Bradley at last allowed himself to be led away.

2

The vicarage of St. Mark's, Southdene, was a big draughty Victorian house, cool on the hottest day, and a horror to heat during a bad winter. The study, the two bedrooms in use, and the kitchen-cum-living-room were little havens of warmth and cheer among the stone-cold passages and arctic stairways.

But most glowing of all was the vicar's daughter herself. Angela Grey was twenty-two, tall, chestnut-haired, and with a face as alive and changeable as a windy sky. She had a quick intelligence and was competent at almost anything she turned her hand to, but after taking her degree she had, like so many of her generation, found it difficult to settle down to a career, nor did she show any inclination to marry. In fact her chief propensity was to keep drifting back home. She would take any old office job in London for a little while, telling her father that she would be staying with friends there, and then she would suddenly turn up at the vicarage again and throw herself with great enthusiasm into the work of the parish, livening up the Youth Club, organizing old people's outings, and writing—anonymously—slightly scandalous but very entertaining articles for the parish magazine.

Nevil regarded her way of life with mixed feelings. Angela was the light of his eyes and to glance out of the study window and see her coming up the drive was his greatest joy. He dreaded losing her, but at the same time he worried a lot because she seemed unable permanently to tear herself away from him. At the time of Maureen Myrtle's death Angela had been home for a longer stretch of time than usual. She had remarked in an offhand manner that there was a man who had not turned out quite what she had expected, and had never referred to it again. Apart from her usual parish activities she found various ways of earning money—home typing, dressmaking, and anything that turned up—and she showed every sign of settling down in Southdene permanently, with every appearance of contentment.

Her father did not quite know what to do. It was an unusual quandary for a parent, to have a child so markedly unwilling to go away. But on the day of Maureen Myrtle's funeral, Nevil's little niggling worry about Angela was far outweighed by his very immediate concern for Clive.

Angela came out of the kitchen and met them in the hall, her mouth open ready to reproach her father for staying out so long in the cold, but she changed her mind when she saw Clive.

"You both look as if you could do with a drink," she said. "In the cupboard in the study, Clive. Could you go and fetch the whisky—and sherry too if there's any left."

When Clive was out of earshot she asked softly: "What's the matter, Papa?"

"I wish you wouldn't call me that," said Nevil irritably.

"I'm going through a Victorian phase. It'll soon be over." Angela hastily set an extra place at the kitchen table and took a dish out of the oven. "Clive looks like a torture-victim," she went on. "What on earth has happened?"

"He had the most ghastly row with Reginald in the churchyard. Clive accused him of murdering his mother."

"Good Lord." Angela stopped in her tracks and stared at her father. "I know Reginald is a revolting creature but surely he wouldn't actually murder anybody."

"I don't know." The vicar sat down wearily at the kitchen table. "It's not entirely impossible, I suppose, that he contrived some sort of overdose. She was dying in any case, and heavily drugged, and he might have hastened the process."

"But the doctor . . ."

"Ssh." Nevil raised his hand to indicate that he could hear Clive approaching. "Could we give him a bed, Angy?" he whispered. "Just for a day or two till the worst is over."

"Of course. It'll have to be the front attic. The back bedrooms are impossible. I'll take one of the oil stoves up after lunch."

"Clive," she said, turning to the boy who had now come into the room carrying a bottle in each hand and looking dazed and bewildered, as one coming back to life after a nightmare, "would you like to stay with us here for a couple of days? It won't be anything like as comfortable as the Old Manor, but it will give you a bit of peace and quiet to get your bearings."

"D'you really mean it?"

Clive put the bottles down on the table and stared at Angela as if he could hardly believe she was real.

"Won't I be a nuisance?"

"Not if you make up your mind not to be. Come on. Eat and drink, both of you. You'll feel better for it."

They helped themselves to beef stew and for a little while few words were spoken. The colour returned to the vicar's face and Clive began to look slightly less hag-ridden. When Angela began to pour boiling water on to the coffee powder, however, Clive pushed his chair back and jumped to his feet and cried in his most agitated manner: "I oughtn't to have stayed. I ought to have gone straight back to the house. It may be too late."

He rushed out of the room. Nevil and Angela caught him up at the front door and grabbed hold of him at either side.

"You're not to go there alone," they said almost in unison.

"Can't you telephone to tell them you're here?" asked Nevil.

"If you've absolutely got to go, I'll run you up in the car," said Angela.

Clive hesitated.

"Hold on a minute," said Angela. "Just let me get a coat."

She ran up the wide staircase two steps at a time, and Clive stood looking after her in the same yearning manner as before. The vicar, watching him anxiously, noticed this, and his own expression changed from pity and concern to something more like fear.

"You're not to wash up, Papa," said Angela when she returned. "You're to have a little snooze in your chair."

But after they had gone Nevil went neither to the kitchen nor to his favourite armchair. He pulled open one of the small drawers in the bureau in the study and took out a little pile of photographs and old letters. From the former he selected a faded, unframed, much-handled portrait, laid it on the open flap of the bureau, and sat down and stared at it for some time. Then he replaced it in the drawer together with the other papers, rested his face on his hands, and muttered to himself: "What to do—in God's name, what to do!"

Meanwhile Angela backed the old green Mini out of the vicarage drive, shot quickly past the church, the village green, the duckpond, three period cottages and Martha's Pantry—much visited by tourists in summer—and then came to an abrupt halt in the long line of traffic waiting for a chance to turn on to the main Brighton road. The Old Manor was at the far end of a steep and narrow lane the other side of this great obstacle of a busy dual carriageway.

"Sorry," she said to Clive. "There's no other way round."

"If only it's not too late," he said yet again.

"Too late for what?"

"To get hold of what Mother left with her solicitor for me before *he* gets hold of it."

It was perfectly plain to Angela that the "he" did not refer to Maureen Myrtle's solicitor. "Why do you think the solicitor may have already come and gone?" she asked as they crept slowly forward.

"Mother said I was to have it as soon as the funeral was over."

"And your stepfather knows about this?"

"I don't think he was meant to, but I'm sure he does."

"But if," went on Angela trying to convince herself as much as to convince Clive, "your mother's solicitor has brought something to the house while you've been at the vicarage, surely nobody else would take it if it was addressed to you?"

Clive merely laughed. Angela glanced sideways at him. He was quite an attractive boy, she thought; rather too thin perhaps, but that was a fault on the right side. Unlike Julius Caesar, she had always felt rather distrustful of men who were running to fat. Her own father, whom she loved more than she could ever imagine loving anyone else, had never been in danger of falling into this fault.

"All right," she said, "so your stepfather is capable of any and every meanness and even crime. I'll grant you that if you like. But solicitors are different. They tend to be rather fussy about things like documents going to the right people. Surely if he found you were not there, he would take away whatever it is untill he could give it to you personally?"

"You'd think so, wouldn't you? So would any civilized person. But you don't know my stepfather. His powers of persuasion are phenomenal. They have already worked wonders with Dr. Jephcott, who is quite a shrewd operator himself and not easily taken in."

Again Angela glanced at Clive. He spoke with intense bitterness and he was evidently in a state of very great anxiety, but the circumstances warranted this, and she did not think he was suffering from persecution mania or any other mental disorder brought on by his mother's death and his hatred of his stepfather. On the other hand she had not, as her father had done, actually seen him together with Reginald. Her job now was to prevent such a meeting if she possibly could.

The big roadway produced a gap in the stream of traffic at last, and they shot across and up the steep lane. Several large cars were standing on the gravel patch in front of the house and Angela weaved in and out of them and pulled up near to the front door.

"Good God!" she cried as Clive produced his key. "They're having a party!"

Sounds of laughter and loud conversation came from the room on their left. "Of course people do often get merry after funerals," said Angela, seeing Clive's hurt and angry face and wishing she had not spoken. "It's a reaction to the strain."

"This one isn't." Clive was very grim. "This is true jubilation. He's got his girl-friend and some of the neighbours in, as well as the gang down from London."

"The solicitor," whispered Angela. "Can you see him?"

They stood in the hall just inside the front entrance. The door of the big room was half-open, but so far nobody within had heard their arrival or noticed their presence; there was too much noise going on.

Clive took a step forward and peered round the door. "Can't see him," he muttered.

"D'you know his car?"

He shook his head. "I barely recognize the man. He's a partner in a firm in Brighton. Mother's not been with them long. She went there because she wanted to deal with strangers instead of with Reggie's firm."

"He might have sent a clerk or a secretary."

"He might," agreed Clive. "That would be even worse. It's no good. I'll just have to go in and ask."

"Wait a moment." Angela grabbed his sleeve. "Wouldn't it be better if I go in alone and say I've come on your behalf and that you're staying with us for a little while? You can slip up to your room and collect a toothbrush. Nobody need know you're here."

"I'm not afraid of him," muttered Clive furiously. "I'm bloody well not going to shelter behind you or your father or anyone else."

"It's not sheltering. It's only common sense. Or better still," went on Angela desperately, fearing that she was going to be no more successful than the vicar had been in keeping the two combatants apart, "would be to telephone the Brighton firm and find out exactly what they are doing about handing whatever it is to you. In fact we ought to have done that before we came. What idiots we are."

"They'll only say they've sent someone out here," said Clive.

"But you don't know for sure. Oh, do let's try phoning first! Is there anywhere in the house we can go where we won't be interrupted?"

Clive appeared to hesitate and Angela's hopes rose. But it was too late. The door of the big drawing-room was pulled right open and Aunt Sarah Delaney stood there, red-faced, obviously having drunk several glasses of champagne, and equally obviously feeling very guilty about it.

"Clive!" she exclaimed for the whole house to hear. "It's you at last. Where on earth have you been? We've been worried to death about you."

"Sorry, Auntie," said Clive, rather to Angela's surprise because she had expected him to make a sarcastic retort. "Are you and Uncle Geoff going now?"

"Well yes, we thought we'd better. It's a long drive, you know."

"A very long journey," agreed Clive gravely. "You'd better delay no longer."

"Clive." Aunt Sarah suddenly became tearful. "I do care about your mother, you know. I do really. I didn't really want all that drink. I don't know how it happened, and neither does Geoffrey. I suppose we ought to have gone away immediately after the funeral service, as Derek and Evelyn did. But it seemed rather rude, and then I missed you and kept hoping you would turn up, and then we got up here and your stepfather . . ."

"Say no more, dear Auntie," said Clive. "I understand perfectly."

"That's all right then," said Aunt Sarah, dabbing at her eyes. "And you won't forget I'm there, will you, and if you'd like to come back with us now . . ."

This less than half-hearted invitation was made with an anxious glance over her shoulder: Geoffrey Delaney, big, pompous and impatient, had joined them in the hall.

"I'm all right, Aunt Sarah," said Clive, leaning forward and kissing her lightly. "I'm staying at the vicarage for a bit. I'll send you my address when I move on."

"Thank you, my dear." Sarah Delaney finishing her mopping-up operations and fumbled in her handbag.

"Hurry up, hurry up," said her husband impatiently. "Women—always fussing with something or other. Goodbye, Clive. Get yourself out of this hothouse place. Get a job. Stand on your own feet. Make a man of you."

He hustled his wife away. Angela and Clive stared at each other for a moment and then suddenly they both burst into laughter.

"He really did say it, he really did say it," murmured Angela.

"I know. He often does. Well, that settles it," added Clive, sobering up as suddenly as he had begun laughing. "I can't keep my presence quiet now. To business."

"Perhaps no one heard your aunt," said Angela doubt-fully.

"You think so?"

"Anyway, no one else seems to be coming out."

"Why should they? They expect me to come in. Will you walk into my parlour, said the spider to the fly. Well, at least it's a big parlour, with plenty of room for the fly to manœuvre, and spiders aren't always so very quick on their feet. Coming to see the fun?"

With a helpless shrug and a feeling of foreboding, Angela followed him into the room.

— 3 —

The big drawing-room at the Old Manor had three long windows. From them one had a fine view of the old village of Southdene in the valley below, with the Downs rising either side and concealing much of the new housing estates, and the line of the sea beyond. Between two of these windows stood a gate-legged table laden with a great variety of savoury and sweet dishes, and between the other window and the door stood a rather smaller table with the drinks. These were being dispensed by Reginald himself, helped by a slim, slight, pretty woman in her late thirties, with a fixed sweet smile on her face and dangerously observant blue eyes.

This was Felicity Westbrook, who had lost two husbands in one way or another, and now lived alone in the cottage half way up the lane. She had a nurse's training, and it was well known in Southdene that she had spent most of her time up at the Old Manor during Mrs. Myrtle's illness. She ignored Clive, who had greeted his stepfather with tolerable restraint and received a curt nod in response, and made her way over to Angela.

"Why, here's the glamour girl from the vicarage! You're looking lovelier than ever, my dear. That windswept style

was created for you. Have you come to deputize for your
honoured father? Such a shame he had to hurry away after
the funeral. What will you drink?"

"Nothing, thanks," replied Angela equally sweetly. "I've
only come along with Clive to collect some of his belong-
ings. He's going to stay with us for a few days. He doesn't
feel quite up to all the jollification here. On account of his
mother's death, you know."

Felicity's eyes narrowed but her effusiveness did not
lessen.

"It is rather awful, isn't it, my dear? I told Reggie so.
One has to provide some sort of refreshment when people
have come a distance, and I don't believe in being too
miserable—do you?—but I think perhaps he has gone a
little bit too far and I can quite understand that Clive feels
a bit out of it. It's very kind of you angels of Christian
charity to take pity on him. But I think it only fair to warn
you—" and here Felicity drew Angela nearer to the window
and made a great show of looking around to check whether
they were being overheard by Clive before she continued in
a perfectly audible voice—"I think you ought to know that
Clive has been behaving extremely oddly lately. Even
allowing for his mother's death, which was very upsetting I
grant you, though personally I do not think that anyone
could reproach me with not helping in every way I could,
and even allowing for the fact that there was rather an
unhealthy relationship between them—Oedipus you know,
it's often worse in the case of an illegitimate child—that still
doesn't completely excuse his behaviour. Reggie thinks he
is suffering from delusions. Paranoia, you know. This
business of believing that everyone is conspiring against
you."

"I know what paranoia means," said Angela calmly,
"and I know that there are occasions when it is perfectly
true that everyone is against you."

"Oh, but my dear—"

Felicity's eyes opened very wide again.

"Excuse me," said Angela, "but I only came here to be of use to Clive if I could."

She edged away from Felicity and joined Clive, who was standing by himself against the wall near to the door. Reginald, after his brief acknowledgment of Clive's presence, had gone off with a tray of drinks to the group gathered round the far window.

"Can't you ask anyone else about the solicitor?" asked Angela in a low voice. She was sure, from the look on his face, that Clive had heard everything Felicity had said, as no doubt he had been intended to.

"Such as who?" he retorted. "Aunt Sarah is the only one I would trust an inch and you saw how the land lay there. She was practically sozzled. He'd done a good job on her."

For a moment or two Angela wondered whether there might not after all be a glimmer of truth in the suggestion that Clive was irrationally and obsessively suspicious of his stepfather. It did seem a little far-fetched to accuse him of feeding champagne to the aunt so that she would not notice any funny business with the solicitor. In any case, Mrs. Delaney had not appeared to be all that drunk, and she very likely knew nothing at all about whatever it was that Clive was supposed to receive.

If indeed Clive was to receive anything. Could it possibly be that Clive had invented the story in order to make Reginald appear even worse than he was? Angela dismissed this disloyal thought almost as soon as it had formed itself, but a little niggling doubt remained and would not quite be stilled.

"You'll just have to ask him then," she said softly, knowing that it was useless to intervene further, and feeling more apprehensive than ever. "I wish you could speak to him outside, though, and not among all this crowd."

"He'll never agree to that," returned Clive. "He loves an audience."

And I suspect that you do too, said Angela to herself. On the other hand, her thoughts ran on, Clive might be wise in tackling Reggie in public rather than alone. The room was now full of Reggie's acquaintances, and on Clive's side there was nobody except Angela herself, but if it came to blows, surely Reginald's people would help in dragging them apart.

It was several minutes before Reginald returned to the drinks table with a tray of empty glasses. He glanced at Clive and Angela, whispered something to Felicity, who nodded and smiled more sweetly than ever, and then came over and said very casually to Clive: "Glad you decided after all to put in an appearance. Not much use standing glowering here, though. There's a couple of literary agents present among the throng. Like to come and meet them and make your talents known?"

Angela found herself wincing on Clive's behalf, and she was surprised at his self-control when he replied. "No, thanks. I'm not looking for patronage at the moment. I've only come to find out whether Mother's solicitor has delivered an envelope or a package for me."

"Reading the will?" Reginald produced a jolly laugh. "My dear fellow, that is a scene that only takes place in novels. A very useful scene, too, if I may be professional for a moment. But there won't be any reading of wills today, nor at any other time. In fact I doubt whether your mother had anything to put into a will."

"I doubt it too," said Clive, and although his voice was still fairly steady, Angela noted with alarm that his hands were clenching into fists at his sides, "in view of your meanness to her," he concluded.

"It was not my intention to remind you," said Reginald, "of the condition that you and your mother were in when I married her, but since you have raised the matter yourself—"

"We were desperate," cried Clive, his voice rising and his composure slipping at last. "She'd no training except as an actress and she couldn't get a job and she was burdened with me. And you came along like Father Christmas and we've both of us never stopped paying for it ever since. You didn't want a wife! You wanted someone to torture! And to get rid of when you were tired of it."

"Clive," said Reginald threateningly, "you remember what I said in the churchyard."

"Please, Clive, please!" begged Angela. "You're wandering from the point. We've only come to fetch that envelope from the solicitor. If it's here. Did anything come for Clive since the funeral?" she asked Reginald.

"My dear Miss Grey." Reggie gave her a charming smile and tried very hard to appear taller than Angela's own five foot eight. "I am so sorry that you should be subjected to this family unpleasantness, particularly when your father has already experienced his share of it this morning. He will no doubt have told you of our young friend's behaviour by the graveside. Even making allowances for the strain of the occasion, it was unnecessarily offensive. It would have been unforgiveable in a normal person, but my stepson is unfortunately not quite normal and I am perfectly prepared to help him to the services of a psychiatrist. I have told him so. I can do no more."

"Did anything come from a firm of solicitors in Brighton?" asked Angela, ignoring this speech and skilfully intercepting Clive's violent motion toward Reginald.

"I don't know. I have been very occupied as a host. We have no resident servants at the moment, and the refreshments were sent in by a catering firm. Mrs. Westbrook has been kind enough to do the necessary setting out and has answered the front doorbell. Perhaps you had better direct your enquiry to her."

Angela did this, calling out loudly to where Felicity stood a few yards away. She was determined not to let go of Clive.

"Sorry, can't hear you!" cried Felicity, cupping a hand round one ear but moving no nearer.

Angela dragged Clive towards the drinks table and repeated the question.

"Oh yes, there was an envelope delivered for Clive
Bradley," said Felicity in an offhand manner. "I think it was
while I was getting the room ready before everyone came
back from the church."

"What did you do with it?" demanded Clive.

He was near the end of his tether. Angela, still gripping
his arm, could feel its trembling.

"I told the boy to leave it on the hall table. It was a boy,
wasn't it? Or was it a girl? D'you know, I really can't
remember," said Felicity with an air of great frankness. "I
was terribly busy and I didn't really take much notice, I'm
afraid."

Angela heard her out, but Clive pulled away as soon as
Felicity began speaking and rushed out of the room.

"It's not there now," he said, coming back a moment
later.

"Isn't it?" said Felicity. "Someone must have put it
somewhere else, then. Perhaps up in your room. Have you
looked?"

"It won't be in my room," shouted Clive, and Reginald,
who had moved nearer to them, made an exaggerated
grimace of pain. "It won't be anywhere in this house where
I can find it," continued Clive. "It'll be where you've
hidden it till you can look at it. You rotten sodding little—"

The rest of his words were lost in general cries of alarm
as he raised an arm and swung it at Reginald. The latter
sidestepped and received only a slight glancing blow, but
several people had rushed across from the group by the
window and some of them caught hold of Clive.

"You see! You see what I mean!" cried Reggie, dabbing
at his cheek with a pale yellow handkerchief. "He's out of
his senses. He's positively dangerous. Chuck him out! Get
him out of my house!"

The people holding Clive looked as if they were about to
do so, but the couple who had been with Reginald at the
funeral stepped forward, both speaking with authority in
spite of their rather slouching appearance.

"You can't do that," said the man. "Let the boy go. It's his home."

"And it's all your fault, Reggie. You were deliberately provoking him," said the woman.

The people who had grabbed hold of Clive let him go and there was a moment of stunned and bewildered silence in which nobody quite knew what to do. It was broken by Reginald's daughter Jill, hurtling across from the far end of the room where she had been entwined with a very amorous young man.

"You little bastard!" she screamed at Clive. "Hitting a man twice your age!"

Her hand came up, and when it was lowered again a dark red line appeared on Clive's cheek where the big enamel ring that she wore had scratched the skin.

There was a little gasp from the watching circle of people and then Angela, along with the others, held her breath. If Clive were to go for Jill, all hell would be let loose. But Jill's blow seemed to have sobered him down. He looked down at her and spoke in quiet tones that held more of wonderment than of fury.

"How strange that you should defend him after what he did to your mother."

Jill burst into tears. Reginald put an arm round her and uttered soothing words. The couple who had intervened to prevent Clive from being ejected, turned to Angela and said: "Come on. Better get him away before any further damage is done."

Between the three of them they dragged Clive out into the hall. The man and woman then looked at each other.

"Shall we, Pete?" asked the woman.

"Okay, Tessa," said the man.

"Would you like to come back to London with us?" said Pete to Clive. "We'll be leaving in a minute or two."

"I—I—" Clive stared at them both, continued to stammer for a moment longer, and then hid his head in his hands.

"It's very kind of you," said Angela, "but honestly I think it would be best if he comes straight back with me. To the vicarage," she added hastily.

The other two nodded. "That would be better," said Tessa.

"As long as somebody is looking after him," said Pete. "You'd better hurry now, or Reggie will be at him again."

Angela needed no urging. This unexpected little piece of kindness from two of Reginald's oldest friends seemed to have stunned Clive completely, so that he allowed himself to be led away unresisting.

Pete and Tessa stood in the porch of the Old Manor House and watched the green Mini wind down the hill towards the main road. They had a small antique shop in Hampstead which brought only a modest income, and they had known Reginald in his early Bohemian days, before he became rich and famous. Jill's mother, Reggie's first wife, had been one of their circle.

"I am wondering," said Pete, "whether we ought not to get Jill away too. There's going to be a violent reaction after what that boy said."

"Odd, isn't it," said Tessa, "that Clive should say that. Hardly tactful. But then I've always found him a bit oafish."

"So would you be if Reggie was determined to make you appear so," said Pete with a touch of grimness.

Tessa looked troubled. "Of course, Reggie has always hated the boy. This Henry the Eighth thing he has got about producing a son of his own in legal matrimony, I suppose."

"With poor Katie as Katherine of Aragon who only provided him with a daughter. A very apt comparison. I thought he had got over it, but the obsession still seems to hold."

"Worse than ever, I imagine," said Tessa. "It must have been salt rubbed in the wound for Reggie to see Maureen with her own son Clive and not to have her produce one of his. What a hellish life they must have led. I wonder if Clive knows about this mania of Reggie's? He obviously knows something, or he wouldn't have said that to Jill. At any rate, one thing is sure: in spite of all these hysterics about Reggie poisoning Maureen, Clive is no more unbalanced than the rest of us."

"I think Clive is probably basically sane," agreed Pete, "but I am seriously beginning to wonder whether Reggie is."

"You mean—" Tessa hesitated. "You mean that Clive may be right about his mother?"

Pete shrugged. "Perhaps that's going too far. Maureen certainly had cancer. I meant the general picture. This solicitor's letter for Clive. How much would you bet that Reggie hasn't got hold of it? Remember how he used to open Kate's letters when he suspected she'd got interested in another man?"

Tessa made a face. "The way we're talking, you'd hardly guess that he was our friend."

"Well, he isn't really, is he? Not now. He's moved out of our sphere. Did you feel happy with that bitching gang of literary lights in there?" And Pete nodded over his shoulder in the direction of the drawing-room.

"Not in the least," said Tessa, "but we had to come, didn't we? Reggie was scared stiff of the funeral service. He's bursting with religious superstition really, however much he tries to pretend he isn't. We couldn't let him down."

"That's it exactly. He clings to us when he is forced to come down to earth. Graveyard earth."

"And what now? Frankly, I've had about enough for the moment."

"So have I."

They glanced at each other, and then with the swift and

silent agreement of people who have spent many years together and are in tune with each other, they moved towards their car.

"What about Jill?" asked Tessa.

"She knows she can come to us at any time," replied Pete.

The party broke up soon after Pete and Tessa had departed. A few people lingered on, doing justice to the remaining food and drink and hoping for more drama, but Jill had returned to the amorous young man in the corner, and Reggie himself ceased to be amusing and became very silent and morose. Felicity Westbrook moved among the remaining guests, chatting brightly, but by this time the party was past saving.

"Ted and I are going into Brighton to have a change from country life," said Jill when there were only the four of them left, the two young people, Felicity, and Reginald. "Can I come back here to sleep if I need to, Dad?"

"You will obviously *need* to sleep at some time or other," replied her father, "and you *may,* if you wish, satisfy that need under this roof."

Jill flushed and bit her lip. "If it's like that, I guess we'll just find some place in Brighton," she said.

"As you wish, child."

Reggie sank down into a chair. He suddenly looked old and tired.

"If you do come back—either or both of you," he went on, "please be so good as to come in quietly. I too feel the need of a night's sleep. Felicity, give them a spare key."

When the two young people had gone, Reginald got up from his chair, yawned, and surveyed the room.

"God, what a mess. Why on earth did we have to have all this gang in?"

"You invited them, Reggie."

"Did I? I've no recollection of doing so. Some of them, yes. But I suspect we've been supplying refreshments to a fair number of gatecrashers. Look at that." He moved wearily over to the drinks table and stared at it in disgust. "Not a single unopened bottle. This is going to cost a bomb."

"Well, you can afford it, can't you?"

Felicity's set sweet smile had vanished at last. She too looked very tired. The high, elegant room was not only stuffy, smoke-laden, and faintly sordid; it was also, at last, empty of all pretence.

"I can't afford to entertain half the scroungers of the neighbourhood," snapped Reginald.

"Are you trying to tell me I ought to have kept people out?"

"Of course not. Don't be so silly, Fizz. And don't, I implore you, go and turn out like all other women and take everything personally. I really did think you were free from that weakness."

Felicity compressed her lips and began to stack some of the dirty plates together.

"Do you have to do that now?" asked Reginald.

"Not if you would prefer to do it yourself," she replied very tartly.

"Oh come on, girl." He moved towards her. "Do you realize that we've got the place to ourselves at last? No long-suffering invalids. No madly-suspicious stepsons. Don't you realize that, you fizzy little sexpot?"

"I was wondering," said Felicity, the smile returning to her lips, "just when you were going to remember it yourself."

But some hours later, when Reginald was lying in the heavy sleep that Felicity had made sure of by slipping a strong sedative tablet into his nightcap of rum and water, she slid quietly out of bed and equally silently crept from the room. It was probably not all that big an envelope, she said to herself, and the jacket of the suit he had been wearing was fairly loose. He could easily have slipped it into an inner pocket and hidden it somewhere when he left the drawing room. But where, where? Felicity stood still at the head of the staircase, one hand resting lightly on the rail. The house was hot, silent, and very dark. Even with Reggie in a drugged sleep, she dared not switch on the landing light. He couldn't possibly wake and find her and yet she was afraid. If ever he found out what she was doing he would murder her. And Felicity herself was not quite sure why she was going to such risks to find out what was in that envelope that the young clerk from the solicitor's office had left for Clive Bradley. All she knew was that Reggie had gone to considerable lengths to get the envelope into his own possession without anybody else knowing. Except for Felicity, and he would certainly not have let her know if he had been able to prevent it.

The solicitor's clerk had asked for Mr. Clive Bradley. Felicity had put him to wait in the dining-room to the right of the front entrance, not wanting him to be mixed up with the guests, and quite genuinely intending to tell Clive when he returned from the funeral. But Clive had not returned, and Reggie, going into the dining-room for some reason or other shortly after he came into the house, must have found the young clerk there. That was all Felicity knew about it until Clive had started asking questions, and Reggie had come over and whispered to her that the envelope for Clive had been left on the table in the hall and she was to tell Clive so.

Well, she thought as she clung to the banisters and made her way slowly downstairs in the dark, she had backed Reggie up on that and on everything else too and hadn't breathed a word about the envelope to anyone. And she was perfectly prepared to swear to his story anywhere if need be, and stand by Reggie, just so long as he treated her fairly, and either married or else made a will in her favour, but if he went back on his promise . . .

Felicity reached the front hall. The little shudder which shook her was due not only to the fact that she wore nothing but a thin nightdress, nor to the fact that even in this overheated house, a little draught came from the front door,

which faced south-west and took the full force of the storms
from over the ocean. She shivered because she was afraid
and was not at all sure, for all her bravado, whether she
would ever have the courage to blackmail Reggie when it
came to the point. However, it would be stupid to neglect
the opportunity to get hold of some weapons for blackmail.

To her right was the door to the big drawing-room. The
stale smell of a party hangover was still faintly noticeable in
the hall. To her left was the door of the dining-room. Had
Reggie hidden the envelope in there, immediately after
persuading the solicitor's clerk to part with it? Felicity
rather thought not. It would be too obvious. He would know
that she could work that out for herself.

No. She felt sure that he had slipped it into his pocket and
placed it somewhere later on, at greater leisure, while the
party was in full swing and he could leave the room without
being noticed.

Perhaps the study was the most likely, and should be her
first place of search. It was a small room beyond the
dining-room, reached from a corridor off which also led the
kitchen and the downstairs cloakroom and various utility
rooms. There was a pleasant outlook over the gardens and
shrubbery and Reggie had a good view of the drive up from
the lane, so that he always knew who was leaving or
approaching the house as he sat at his desk.

Felicity felt her way along the corridor and pushed open
the study door. The curtains had not been drawn and her
eyes, accustomed by now to the darkness, could make out
the dim shapes of furniture in the faint light that came from
the window. She crept into the room and for a moment her
breath left her as she thought she could see the shape of
Reggie's head and shoulders bent over the desk. But it was
only the high back of the chair, standing at a slight angle to
the desk. Felicity took a firm grip on herself and reached out
for the Anglepoise lamp. Her nerves could stand no more
shadows, and in any case she would find nothing without
the light on.

She sat down at the desk and tried the drawers. None of them was locked. It would hardly be here, then, although it might as well be to make sure while she had the chance. Deftly and systematically she began to search. First the drawers, then the top of the desk, then the filing cabinet. Nothing was to be found but stationery, letters and documents concerning Reginald's writings, proof copies of novels, and a rough draft of the book on which he was now engaged. Reggie was a careful and fastidiously tidy worker. It made the search easier in one way, more difficult in another. There was little chance that he had slipped the envelope carelessly among some other papers, trusting that it would not be noticed in the general muddle. Reggie was very thorough in all he did and took no chance that could possibly be avoided.

Felicity shut up the filing cabinet and sat down once more at the desk to think. What next? Her mind was so intent on her problem that she failed to listen for any sounds in the house and was taken completely by surprise when she heard the footsteps in the corridor. They stopped at the study door and sent her jumping to her feet, a quivering bundle of nerves, clutching her nightgown around her and wondering in horror whether she had given Reggie the wrong tablet.

The door of the study was pushed open. Felicity clung to the side of the desk and looked up. Her jaw dropped in a mixture of amazement and relief.

"What the hell do you think you are doing here?" demanded Reginald's daughter Jill.

Felicity had completely forgotten, in all the excitements of the day, that there was a possibility that Jill might return to the house. She goggled at her stupidly.

Jill came forward into the room. She was still dressed in the jeans and sloppy sweater that she had been wearing all day. Her heavy dark hair was straggling over her face and she looked cold and unhappy as well as angry.

"I didn't hear you come in," said Felicity, pulling her face together and achieving a parody of her usual smile.

"You weren't meant to. Father made it plain enough that I had to be quiet."

"It's good of you to take so much notice of your father's wishes," gushed Felicity. "So unlike most young people nowadays."

"Oh, cut out the syrup!" cried Jill impatiently. "And just tell me what the game is, sneaking round the study at this hour."

"Ssh." Felicity looked anxiously towards the door. "You might wake him."

"I hope I do. I reckon he ought to know. I reckon I ought to go and fetch him right now."

Felicity, now beginning to recover herself, took no notice of this threat. First of all, she knew that for all Jill's bluster, the girl was at heart a little afraid of Reginald. Secondly, Jill was as human as anybody else when it came to being inquisitive.

"I believe that your father has taken an envelope that came for Clive from his mother's solicitor," she said, "and has hidden it somewhere in here. I wondered what was in it, that was all."

This, as she had calculated, was much more effective than any self-defence or further attempts at flattery would have been. Jill's curiosity was awakened and she softened visibly as she came towards the desk.

"From Clive's mother's solicitor," she repeated. "I wonder what it can be."

"Will you help me look for it if I tell you all I know about it?"

Jill did not hesitate for long. She had not, as Clive had said, much reason to be grateful to her father. On the other hand, her mother was dead, she had quarrelled with all her mother's relatives and with most of her own friends, and she led a restless and dissatisfied life, shifting from man to man and from job to job with monotonous frequency. Her father provided some sort of anchor and occasionally he made a great show of giving her an expensive present.

When Clive had attacked Reggie, Jill's impulse to spring to the defence had been perfectly genuine as far as it went. But it was Clive's remark about her mother that had really cut Jill to the core and re-awakened memories that she spent much of her life trying to suppress. She could not forgive Clive for this. If there was any way of getting her own back on him she would gladly take it. She didn't much care for Felicity, but then she didn't much care for anyone, and if she had to have yet another stepmother, at least Felicity was free from encumbrances like children and was less snivelling, than Maureen Myrtle had been. It might be quite a good idea to play along with Felicity; or at any rate pretend to do so.

"Okay," she said, propping herself up against the side of the desk. "Spill the beans."

Felicity did so.

— 5 —

Clive didn't speak a word while Angela was driving him back to the vicarage, and very few once they arrived there. Nevil produced pyjamas and toothbrush, and Angela showed him the meagre attractions of the front attic.

"D'you want to rest now?" she asked.

This did awaken a little flicker of response. He had scarcely slept, it seemed, since his mother's death four days previously. Angela left him as warm and comfortable as possible before joining her father in the study. There she gave an account of the events at the Old Manor, to which Nevil listened in silence, and when she had finished he said: "We can soon check on the solicitor by phoning him."

"I don't know which firm it is, and I don't think we ought to disturb Clive now to ask him," replied Angela.

"All right. We'll do it in the morning. In any case the office is probably closed by now."

"And there's another thing." Angela hesitated a moment. "I hate saying this, but I'm sure you'd have felt the same if you'd been there. There's no doubt at all that both Reginald and the Westbrook woman were out to make Clive as miserable as possible, but I still think he may be exaggerating the extent to which everybody is against him. His aunt

36

isn't a bad old thing and she really was worried, and the couple who helped get him out of the house were nice people. And I didn't like what he said to Jill."

"No." Nevil looked very unhappy. "But he had great provocation."

"And so did she. I wouldn't like to answer for my actions if I looked up and saw some tough young man taking a swipe at you, whether or not I had been listening to what led up to it."

"Dear Angy." The vicar smiled faintly.

"All right, so we know Reggie is a stinker, but he is Jill's father, after all."

Nevil stared into the fire for a little while, holding up a hand to shade his eyes from the lamplight. "So you think Clive may show some signs of persecution mania?" he said at last. "It would hardly be surprising. His life has been far from happy. He was devoted to his mother, and her death is a terrible blow."

"Oh I know, I know!" cried Angela. "I loathe suggesting this, and I loathe agreeing with Reginald in anything, but I can't help feeling that the psychiatrist idea isn't such a very bad one. At any rate he needs to talk to some sort of understanding person. Can't you do something about it yourself? You've done some very effective counselling work in the parish and I'm sure Clive would take some notice of you. At least he wouldn't suspect you of having any evil intentions towards him."

The vicar drew in his breath sharply and then tried to turn it into a cough, but Angela, always very observant of her father's reactions, had already noticed the look of pain.

"What's the matter, Papa?" she asked. "Why don't you want to help Clive? I thought you did. Rescuing him after the funeral like that."

Nevil dropped his hand from his face, looked straight at Angela, and said very firmly: "Once for all, Angy, will you stop calling me papa. I don't like it."

"All right." She thought a moment. "I know. I'll have a

nineteen-thirties phase—all slinky and Eton-cropped—and
call you pater."

"That was the nineteen-twenties."

"Was it? Never mind. You're evading the question. Why
don't you want to do one of your well-known pastoral jobs
on Clive? Why not, Pa—, I mean, why not, Dad?"

"I've seen rather a lot of the family over the last few
months. A stranger might approach the problem with a
fresher eye."

"You're still evading the question," said Angela, looking
at him steadily.

Nevil turned to stare into the glowing fire again.

"Do you feel at all attracted towards him, Angy?" he
asked at last in a low voice.

"Oh that's it, is it!" cried Angela, looking at her father's
averted face with compassionate amusement. "You're
afraid he's going to steal my affections—this stranger
you've taken within your gates. You poor old thing. I rather
thought all the self-sacrificing stuff about marrying me off
to a curate was too good to be true. You don't really want
me to marry and leave you, Dad, do you, whatever you
say?"

"I do want you to marry and I shall have to put up with
your leaving me," replied Nevil. "And I'm perfectly
serious about this, so please don't laugh, Angy. I really
want to know: is there any likelihood that you are going to
fall in love with Clive?"

"Can anyone guarantee that they will never fall in love?"
countered Angela. "There's lots of men I've been attracted
to. Some of them you know and some of them you don't. I
could even go for Reggie himself if I let myself. I don't like
plump men, but there's a horrible fascination about him—a
sort of demon lover appeal. And I've no doubt that I shall
fall in love with a frightful crash one day, since nobody
seems to escape it." She paused a moment before continuing. "In fact I recently took a bit of a tumble, as you've no
doubt guessed, though of course you've been too tactful to

mention it. Whether it has inoculated me against future infections I can't yet say, but I can truthfully tell you that I feel nothing for Clive Bradley except a mixture of pity and exasperation and I think it very unlikely that these feelings will ever change to any great extent. For one thing, he's terribly immature for his age."

"Yes, I'm afraid he is," agreed Nevil, almost as if he were apologizing for Clive.

Angela looked at him curiously. "Well, that's not your fault, Dad. I suppose he'll grow up one day. And in any case, it's not only Clive that's worrying you, is it? I believe you've been brooding over Mother again."

Nevil admitted that he had indeed been thinking a lot that day about Angela's mother, who had died when the girl was fifteen, shortly after their removal from London to Southdene.

"Having guilt feelings, I suppose," said Angela. "Though heaven knows why. If Mother wasn't happy she had only herself to blame."

"Not really, my dear. She had been brought up in a very comfortable home. When she married me she had no idea that I was going to go into the Church and turn into a poor parson."

"For better, for worse," said Angela.

"Well yes, but there was an awful lot of worse from her point of view. I sometimes think we ought to alter the marriage service drastically or else abolish it altogether. It's asking a bit much to make two people commit themselves to each other for life in all circumstances. It's only encouraging selfishness on the one hand and an unhealthy self-sacrifice on the other."

"Dad!" Angela looked surprised and even a trifle shocked. "I thought I knew you, but I never knew you felt like this. I shall tell Ronnie on you when he gets back. He'll probably think it his duty to write to the Bishop."

Ronnie Fenwick was the curate who was at present absent on the occasion of his sister's wedding. He was a hardworking young man with a great sense of vocation, and he wavered between admiration for Nevil and disapproval of the vicar's occasional unconventional and unclerical behaviour. Angela, of course, he had worshipped from the first, and she liked him as much as she had liked any of her father's curates.

"Can it be," she continued, trying to cheer her father up, "that you are 'having doubts,' like the clergyman hero of a Victorian novel?"

"I don't know," said Nevil in a dead voice. "I don't know anything at all."

"I do," cried Angela, jumping to her feet. "I know that you're worn out and are going to be cosseted for the rest of the evening, and when young Clive wakes up I'll keep him away from you. Though I don't think," she added, coming over to Nevil's chair and inspecting him closely, "that you are really going to be any the worse for this morning's activities. There's coughs and coughs, and I suspect a touch of the histrionic art in this one. Besides, you're quite a tough old devil really, for all that lean medieval-saintly appearance. You've got something on your mind, and you're not being honest with me about it, but I won't pester you any more at the moment. In fact I'm feeling more than a trifle jaded myself. Trying to stop Clive bashing Reggie about is a terribly exhausting occupation. I hope he's finished with breathing vengeance for the rest of the day."

This hope, at least, was realized. Clive woke up and ate a little supper in a dazed manner and then relapsed into unconsciousness again. The vicar shut himself up with his books and his thoughts and Angela got out the portable typewriter and the vast manuscript of a doctoral thesis on the fiscal policies of the inter-war governments, and settled down to work at the kitchen table. It was a terribly boring job, but it was well-paid, and it had the advantage of only occupying her fingers and her eyes and the surface of her mind, so that as she worked, she could mull over the events of the day.

Angela found them rather disquieting. That her father should go out of his way to comfort someone in Clive's position was by no means uncommon. Distraught and unhappy people were liable to turn up at the vicarage at all hours and Nevil would always do what he could to help. Angela resented her father being what she termed exploited, but at the same time she would have hated him to act other than in pity and charity. And she had to admit that for the most part her father never allowed himself to be too much weighed down by the burden of other people's troubles; having sent the sufferer away calmer, and usually with something to hope for, he would then shake it all off with an air of almost cynical detachment.

But today it had been quite different. The vicar seemed to have become deeply and personally involved in this business of Clive and his stepfather and was taking it to heart to a most unusual degree. Angela continued to puzzle over it after she went to bed. On the bedside table stood a photograph that was very precious to her—a picture of her parents on their wedding-day. Whenever she went away, even if only for a few days, Angela always took this photograph with her. She picked it up now and studied it earnestly for a while. They had never been a demonstrative family, for all the deep currents of feeling that ran between them. Nostalgic grieving over the past was never encouraged by Nevil, and photographs and other sentimental souvenirs were few and far between in the household. Angela sometimes wondered that her father kept no picture of her mother on show, but she would never have dreamed of reproaching him for the omission.

She knew the bare facts of her parents' courtship and marriage; she knew that it had been a heavy blow to her mother when her father decided to give up his former profession and take orders, and she knew, from her own experience, that there had been great strains in the marriage thereafter and that her father still suffered from time to time from the gnawing feeling that he had caused unhappiness.

Could it possibly be, she wondered, that there was some
link-up with the Myrtle household that had aroused painful
memories? Mrs. Myrtle had come to church fairly regularly
before her illness confined her to the house. She had played
a small part in parish activities, and appeared to be a
well-meaning, though rather dim and ineffectual person.
Angela had felt vaguely sorry for her, since she didn't
appear to take any pleasure in her role as wife of a celebrity,
and when Clive appeared on the scene, after what had
apparently been a not very successful attempt to strike out
for himself in journalism in Fleet Street, it was immediately
obvious to everybody in the village that the situation at the
Old Manor was a far from happy one.

Angela noticed that her father always seemed very tired
and depressed after visiting Mrs. Myrtle, but she attributed
this to the effort of trying to calm down the passions in that
household, and to the strain of being polite to Reginald,
whom he had disliked from the first. She had rather hoped,
after Maureen Myrtle's death, that they would not have to
see any more of the Old Manor people. Clive never came to
church, and although Reginald came now and then, as a sort
of insurance policy to be on the safe side, he was not likely
to want to be on close visiting terms with the vicarage.

But the moment she saw her father bringing the stricken-
looking Clive into the house after the funeral, Angela had
realized that this hope had been in vain. They were landed
with the problem, both of them, for better or for worse. She
would help him, but he would have to tell her the truth; and
she had no doubt that he would, for her father would never
let her down. Unlike so many men, who from cowardice or
from a mistaken notion of being kind, kept from you things
that you would much rather have known at once.

As Gary had done. And Angela's thoughts returned for a
while to their own private hurt. Gary had known perfectly
well that she didn't want to marry him. It was not that that
had upset her so much when she discovered he had a wife.
It was the realization that there was a big and important area

of his life and thoughts about which she knew nothing, that had been deliberately kept hidden from her during all the time she had believed that they had each other's perfect confidence. That was the hurt—not the fact itself, but the not being trusted with it. And Gary had never understood. It was stupid of her, Angela thought, and also jealous and possessive, to want to feel that someone you cared for trusted you completely, but she couldn't help it; that was the way she was made.

Well, she was getting over it, although it had been a nasty toss, and it was a great comfort to know that her father would always remain the rock he had always been, and that he, at least, would never let her down by allowing her to stumble upon some secret knowledge that had been withheld from her.

It never occurred to Angela that she herself might be accused of secrecy. Had it done so, she would have responded to the accusation with a deep irrational feeling that went against her conscious intelligence; a feeling that while youth had a right to secrecy, middle-age had no such right. Middle-age was there to be relied on or rebelled against; not to produce startling revelations about itself.

So Angela and her father, each of whom loved the other more than anyone else in the world, pursued their unspoken and lonely thoughts throughout much of the night, while Clive lay in a restless, feverish sleep. The next morning the vicar of St. Mark's looked much more at peace with himself, as if he had fought with giants during the night and slain them and was ready to face whatever fresh trial might befall. But Clive remained in a bad way. Angela took his temperature and found it much raised.

"If we get Dr. Jephcott," she said, "we can kill two birds with one stone and find out whether he has any suspicions about Clive's mother's death."

"Yes, I was going to talk to him about it," said Nevil. "I'll stay in till he comes. There are no urgent visits to make this morning."

He seemed to be treating the whole affair in a much more normal way, and Angela began to wonder whether her own imagination had been playing tricks when she suspected her father of a more than common interest in Clive's situation. It seems to be catching, she said to herself, all this high drama and accusation and counter-accusation; maybe Dad was worried for some quite different reason. And she resolved to let things take their course for the time being.

Dr. Jephcott was very reassuring all round. He was rather like a modified version of Reginald Myrtle to look at— stocky, not very tall, and with the air of a prosperous man somewhat running to seed.

"Sheer exhaustion and nervous strain," he said after examining Clive. "There's a lot of 'flu around but it's no sort of infection. The lad has had enough. Bit unbalanced at the best of times, you know—bit of a psychiatric history, but we won't go into that just now. Let him sleep round another twenty-four hours and he'll be all right. I'll leave some sedative tablets in case he gets troublesome and starts running amok again."

He leant over the desk in the study to write out a prescription and behind his back Angela and her father glanced at each other. Clive was indeed causing a lot of trouble, but nevertheless neither of them liked the condescending manner in which Dr. Jephcott had spoken: it smacked too much of Clive's stepfather.

"A new drug," said Dr. Jephcott handing over the slip of paper. "Very useful in mental hospitals as a rapid-acting tranquilliser. Mustn't be given in heart cases—could be dangerous there—but otherwise no side effects. And we don't need to worry about our young friend upstairs. Heart's as sound as a bell. Physically, at any rate." And he directed a faintly leering look at Angela and produced a little laugh.

"Thank you," said Nevil taking the prescription. "It will be useful to have these handy. Are you in a hurry? Will you wait for a cup of coffee? Or sherry?"

The doctor accepted the sherry, which just held out, and

Angela did rapid mental calculations about the next week's housekeeping money while Nevil tactfully introduced the subject of Maureen Myrtle's death. There was no point in trying to hide the fact that Clive had accused his stepfather of killing her, since the verger and the gravedigger had overheard everything, and they were both married men and could scarcely be expected to keep this interesting item of gossip to themselves.

"My dear fellow," said Dr. Jephcott in a manner that was again reminiscent of Reginald, "the story was all round the village by tea-time yesterday, in an extraordinary variety of versions. One old lady had Mr. Myrtle choked to death by the side of his late wife's grave."

"Ah well," said Nevil resignedly, "I shall no doubt hear several more when I go the rounds this afternoon. Let's hope it will be a less than nine days' wonder. It won't do either the boy or his stepfather any good if people go on and on about it. Fortunately we've got Colonel Fairchild's daughter getting married next week. To a pop singer, of all things—but a very respectable one. It's going to be a sumptuous affair and it should take people's minds off Myrtle and Clive."

Angela, listening to her father, marvelled anew at his capacity for adapting himself to people and for slipping into the role that made contact with them most fruitful, without in any way sacrificing his own essential integrity. Dr. Jephcott chatted for a little longer, very man to man, very superior about village gossips.

"I suppose," said Nevil casually as Dr. Jephcott got up to go, "that there couldn't conceivably be any basis for Clive's suspicion? No question of a mercy killing, I mean. I imagine you must come across that occasionally in cancer cases. I do hope you don't think I'm being interfering in asking this. The subject happens to be of interest to me, and very relevant to certain aspects of my job."

Dr. Jephcott, who had frowned when Nevil began to speak, looked cheerful again and resumed his easy flow.

"Oh yes, of course. Euthanasia and all that. Naturally you would take an interest in it. Very interested myself, as a matter of fact, though I can't say I entirely agreed with the Archbishop's latest intervention. As a matter of fact I'm drafting a sort of answer to it now. I write a bit on medical matters—nothing academic, just popular stuff, you know, but people seem to like it. Of course it all has to be under a pseudonym. We aren't allowed the luxury of literary fame."

And he gave a self-deprecating little laugh.

"You are not anonymous in this household," said Nevil. "Angela has a friend who contributes to the same journal as you do yourself. So we know your alias. A household name, if I may say so."

Dr. Jephcott turned to beam at Angela, who before shifting her glance from her father, had detected in Nevil's eye just the faintest suggestion of a wink.

"Really?" said Dr. Jephcott. "What is your friend's name?"

They chatted for a moment or two about their mutual acquaintance. You may model yourself on Reginald, Angela was saying to herself as she smiled at him complacently, but you haven't a fraction of his fatal fascination and you never will have.

"I'm interested in the subject of mercy killing too," she said, and watched Dr. Jephcott remove his smile and compose his face into suitable gravity. "I'll be interested to read what you write. You did say, didn't you, that there was no question of it in Mrs. Myrtle's case?"

"No question at all. Can't think how the boy can have got hold of the idea. Perfectly simply case. Very sad, of course, but no particular complications. Mrs. Westbrook did a lot of the nursing—trained nurse—very competent, would trust her anywhere. And the nurse from the agency who came in the last few weeks was equally above reproach. She had my authority to increase the pain-relieving dosage if necessary and she used it on several occasions. Nothing out of the ordinary there."

He moved towards the door.

"Thank you for being so helpful and explicit," said Nevil, accompanying him. "And please forgive me for having asked what must have appeared a rather impertinent question. It will be useful for me to be quite definite in my own mind, in case the matter should crop up again, that Mr. Reginald Myrtle at no time had access to any drugs that were being used to relieve the condition of his wife."

"No, no. That's not quite true," said Dr. Jephcott, pausing at the front door. His voice sounded strangled. The struggle between his grand social manner on the one hand and his conscience as a man and a doctor on the other was both funny and painful to watch. "It isn't usual," he said after a little convulsive swallow, "to take the precaution of locking all drugs away from the patient's nearest relatives. In fact in most cases it is the nearest relatives who have to administer the drugs. One cannot go about suspecting them all the time. Of course Mr. Myrtle knew what was being prescribed for his wife. Of course he knew where the drugs were kept. He even gave her a tablet himself once or twice, to my certain knowledge. For heaven's sake, Vicar, that doesn't make him a murderer!"

"Of course not," Nevil soothed him down. "I am not suggesting it for a moment. I am sorry that you have distressed yourself by thinking that I was. All I wanted was the ammunition with which to refute any such suggestion."

"Well, you've got it," said Dr. Jephcott. "I've just told you. There is nothing in the least bit suspicious about Mrs. Myrtle's death. I'll stake my whole professional reputation on that. They can dig her up and take her to pieces tomorrow if they like and they won't find anything amiss. Good God, if people start questioning my death certificates—!"

"Dr. Jephcott," said Nevil with warmth, "please believe me when I say that I understand entirely how you feel. I am in much the same position myself when it comes to professional reputation and public opinion."

The doctor made an effort to pull himself together. "Yes. Yes, of course you would be, Vicar," he said.

"I promise you that I am the very last person to be party to any such insinuations against yourself and if I ever heard anything of the sort—which I haven't—I should stamp on it at once."

"Thank you. Yes, yes, of course." Dr. Jephcott mopped his brow. "Forget all about it. Sorry, stupid of me," he was heard to mutter as Nevil accompanied him to his car. "Don't like this sort of thing—highest respect for Reginald Myrtle—very good writer as well as very popular one."

Nevil got rid of him at last.

—6—

"Bloody little pompous ass!" exploded the vicar of St. Mark's when he returned to where Angela was waiting in the study.

Angela gave a shout of laughter and flung up her hands in mock horror. "Shame on you! I'll tell Ronnie."

Nevil laughed too. "Well, we aren't going to get much further there," he said. "There's no point in asking Mrs. Westbrook, and even if we track down the agency nurse she won't tell us the truth. They'll clam up together, the whole lot of them, and blind us with medical science."

"D'you think Dr. Jephcott was telling the truth?"

Nevil thought for a moment before replying. "Let me put it this way," he said at last. "Whether or not Dr. Jephcott suspects there was anything suspicious about Mrs. Myrtle's death, he is quite sure that nothing can ever be proved."

"Then why was he in such a jitter?"

"Because of my enquiries, I suspect. He is afraid I may encourage Clive to persist in his accusations."

"And while Clive can be shrugged off as being hysterical and revengeful and possibly even mentally unbalanced, an accusation from the vicar of St. Mark's would have to be taken seriously," said Angela. "Are you going to encourage

Clive to persist in his accusations, by the way?" she added lightly, but at the same time giving her father a very searching look.

"Personally I wish he would drop them," replied Nevil, "but he is certainly not going to rest until he tracks down the letter that his mother wanted him to have. One can hardly blame him for that, at any rate."

"No, I suppose not. After all, if it was addressed to him . . . You saw quite a bit of Mrs. Myrtle," went on Angela, still closely watching her father. "Have you any notion what could be in Clive's letter?"

"I did see quite a lot of her," agreed Nevil, "but she did not tell me what she was proposing to leave for Clive after her death."

The careful phrasing of this reply did not escape Angela's notice. She was quite sure now that her father was not being open with her, and this was very hurtful. Such a thing had never happened before; nothing had ever occurred to lessen the perfect trust that existed between them. However much she tried to tell herself that it was not Clive's fault, she could not help feeling resentful against Clive, and at the same time guilty about feeling resentful, and to assuage this guilt she began to busy herself on Clive's behalf.

"I'm going up to see if he's awake," she said, "and ask him the name of that solicitor."

She returned a few minutes later to say that Clive had woken up and looked much less feverish and more peaceful. He had talked quite rationally and answered her questions before dozing off again. "So we can settle that one straight away," she said, going over to the telephone that stood on the vicar's open bureau.

"Baslow and Snailes? May I speak to one of the partners, please?"

A sleepy girl's voice the other end told her that everybody was in conference with clients and would she ring again after lunch at three o'clock, please, caller.

"The dozy Doris!" cried Angela, putting the receiver

back with a little slam of impatience. "Does she mean phone at three or do they have lunch at three?"

"I'll get my own business over quickly and be back to phone myself," promised Nevil.

But it was nearly half past four before the sleepy receptionist in a little office overlooking the Royal Pavilion gardens in Brighton pressed the switch that connected with the larger office above and said: "Vicar of Southdene on the line to you, Mr. Baslow. Will you take the call?"

"The Vicar of Southdene," repeated Mr. Baslow, glancing across the desk at the young articled clerk who had recently joined the firm.

"That's what I said, Mr. Baslow," said the girl with a sort of lazy cheekiness.

"All right," snapped the senior partner. "Put him through. No, don't go away, John. Southdene. May be something to do with that Myrtle business. Good afternoon, sir, what can I do for you?" he said into the receiver in a very different tone of voice. And then he listened for a little while and the young clerk sat anxiously doodling round the edges of a much-amended draft of a will.

"Yes, yes indeed," said Mr. Baslow at last. "One of my staff did deliver a personal communication addressed to Mr. Clive Bradley at the Old Manor, Southdene, at approximately one-thirty yesterday afternoon. I sent him over in the lunch-hour. We are exceptionally busy here at the moment and there was nobody else free to come."

At the other end of the wire Angela, standing close enough to her father to hear what was being said down the telephone, cried: "Strewth! Busy! They're all asleep!" and then clapped a hand over her mouth as Nevil frowned at her.

"Would it be troubling you too much," said Nevil, "to ask you a question or two about the actual delivery of the letter to Mr. Bradley?"

Angela mimed a little gesture of applause. In the Brighton office Mr. Baslow, with the air of someone washing his hands of the whole affair, said: "I think you'd best speak to my clerk yourself, Vicar. He's here in the room with me now. I'll hand him the phone."

The two in the vicarage heard the sound of movement, and then a young and very nervous voice said: "John Martin speaking, sir. What was it you wanted to know?"

"I'm afraid I may be troubling you at an inconvenient moment," said Nevil kindly. "The fact is that we have Mr. Bradley here with us—he has been taken rather ill, I'm afraid—and he is very worried about something to do with his mother's estate and I have promised to try to sort it out for him. Would it be too much to ask you to come out to Southdene this afternoon after you leave work? Do you have a car? If not, my daughter could easily come in to Brighton and pick you up."

"Well, I don't know that I can be much help—well, that's awfully kind of you, sir," stammered John Martin under the suspicious and unfriendly eye of Mr. Baslow. "Well, actually I do have a car and I'm not doing anything in particular this evening and I know Southdene quite well as a matter of fact because the curate is an old school friend of mine."

"That's settled then," said Nevil. "We'll look forward to meeting you."

"Good Lord," said the boy in the office in a dazed manner as he replaced the receiver. "That was funny. He wants me to go over there to discuss Mrs. Myrtle's estate. But there's practically nothing in the estate, is there?"

"You ought to know," said Mr. Baslow. "You drafted the will. It is, you will remember, very straightforward. I do not imagine that even you will find any difficulty in answering whatever query should happen to arise. As for that other matter, please try to remember that nobody in this office has the least idea of what was contained in the sealed envelope that was to be delivered to Mr. Bradley."

"No, sir, of course not," said John Martin.

In the vicarage study Angela said to her father: "Do we really want to have this boy with us the whole evening? If he's a friend of Ronnie's we shall never get rid of him. They'll be two of a kind."

"I'm sorry," said Nevil, "but I could see no way to avoid it. The poor boy has obviously made a bit of a bloomer and it would have been too unkind to force him to confess it with his boss breathing down his neck. This seemed the only way out on the spur of the moment."

"So you have to be careful of his feelings too!" cried Angela, all her own feelings of resentment and suspicion suddenly swelling up into a great fury against her father. "Don't you realize how hopeless it makes things for me, you being so damned kind and understanding and bloody perfect in every way!"

And she rushed out of the room and slammed the door. Nevil looked after her in unhappy bewilderment for a moment, and then he sat down at the desk, pulled out a sheaf of invoices and estimates and other papers dealing with the church repairs, and studied them carefully, making notes from time to time.

In the event John Martin did not stay at the vicarage for the whole evening, although he looked at first as if he intended to do so. Nevil and Angela drank coffee with him and made a little suitable conversation about the coincidence of his knowing the curate. Then the visit to the Old Manor was mentioned.

"Of course I would have preferred to hand the envelope over to Mr. Bradley in person," said the young clerk, "but I had no specific instructions not to give it to anybody else, and when Mr. Myrtle came and said he would hand it on I naturally thought that would be all right."

"Naturally," said both Angela and Nevil without the least hint of sarcasm.

"It was all right, wasn't it?" asked the boy anxiously. "I mean, Mr. Myrtle did hand it on, didn't he?"

The other two very deliberately refrained from exchanging glances and Angela thought it best to let her father reply.

"As far as you personally, and indeed as far as your firm

is concerned, it is perfectly all right," said Nevil in his kindest manner. "Mrs. Myrtle's instructions appear to have been faithfully carried out and that is all you need worry about."

"Then why," asked John, who was very young and nervous and naive but not so naive as all that, "have you had to ask me about it all?"

"Oh dear." This time Nevil did glance at his daughter. "I'm afraid there's been some sort of family argument— there often is after a death unfortunately—and the letter has got mislaid. Everybody is accusing everybody else of taking it. Heaven knows where it has got to now, but since I have unwittingly become involved in it, I thought it would be helpful to get the matter quite clear from your end before plunging in any further. You don't, I suppose, know what the envelope contained?"

"I'm afraid not," said John Martin, looking at Angela and thinking what a lucky devil Ronnie Fenwick was to be working closely with the father of this gorgeous-looking girl. "It came to us through the post, in a sealed envelope marked 'Strictly Private and Personal—to be opened only by Clive Bradley after his mother's funeral,' and enclosed in another envelope with a covering letter from Mrs. Myrtle."

After a few enquiries about times and dates, Nevil said: "I believe I might have posted that to you myself. On one occasion when I visited Mrs. Myrtle in her illness she asked me if I would drop some letters into the postbox for her. I did not notice any of the addresses, but I remember that one of them was quite a large thick envelope and I had to fold it over before it would go in."

"That's right," cried the visitor excitedly. "The sealed envelope did look a bit creased so you must have folded it too when it was inside the bigger one. How extraordinary to think you actually had it in your hands and now you are asking me about it!"

"Very extraordinary," said Nevil drily, and Angela,

seething with curiosity and exasperation, did not know whether to admire his composure or to resent it.

"And nobody in your firm has the least idea of what was in the sealed envelope?" continued Nevil.

"Well, they are not supposed to," said John Martin with the air of one who might perhaps have something a little startling to say, if pushed to it.

It was at this most tantalizing moment that Clive Bradley suddenly burst into the room and recoiled when he saw that a stranger was present.

"Sorry," he mumbled. "Ought to've knocked. Only I woke up and felt miles better and I wondered if there was anything to eat."

"Of course," said Angela, getting up hurriedly. "Come along to the kitchen."

But she was too late. John Martin, who had unfortunately remembered that the vicar had told him Mr. Bradley was ill and staying with them, put two and two together, and with the very natural desire of showing off his own efficiency on behalf of his client, turned to Clive and asked if he was Mr. Bradley.

"Yes." Clive paused in the doorway. "Why do you ask? Who are you, anyway?"

"John Martin of Baslow and Snailes, solicitors of Brighton. Your mother was a client of ours. We shall be getting in touch with you shortly about her estate. Should we address letters to you here or to the Old Manor?"

Clive stared at him with smouldering eyes. His long rest appeared to have done nothing except restore his physical vigour. The resentment and aggression were as active as ever.

"Did you take a letter to the Old Manor addressed to me?" he demanded.

Angela made a gesture of helplessness. Nevil scratched his head and gritted his teeth.

"Why yes, I've just been explaining," said the young

clerk. "I gave it to Mr. Myrtle. He said he would give it to you as soon as you got home."

This, as was only to be expected, led to an explosion from Clive, and the ensuing scene was very disagreeable to all concerned, with the possible exception of Clive himself. Eventually the solicitor's clerk was got off the premises still in one piece, and Angela stirred one of the sedative tablets prescribed by Dr. Jephcott into a strong cup of sweet tea and gave a sigh of relief when Clive gulped it down without noticing any unusual taste. The drug must have been potent, because Clive very soon quieted down and they were able to dissuade him from rushing off to have another go at Reginald straight away.

"We shall get nowhere by violence," said Nevil with great authority. "I must absolutely insist, Clive, that you keep out of the way and let me handle this. I am going to telephone the Old Manor and make an appointment to see your stepfather. Either this evening, or tomorrow morning. Will you kindly leave me in peace to do this. It is not helping me in the least to have you breathing fire and brimstone round the room."

Clive muttered his thanks and promised to keep out of it, and then once again he sat down to a meal prepared by Angela and ate it in almost total silence. When he had finished, however, he managed a smile and said: "You're not a bad cook, are you, Angy? That was super."

"I do my best to give satisfaction," said Angela in a mock-servile voice to camouflage her sudden flare-up of irritation with Clive. It is not his fault, she kept telling herself, that something has gone so horribly wrong between Dad and me; I must stop blaming Clive for it.

She did her best to keep up the light-hearted back-chat while they washed up, but after a while Clive became moody again and wanted to go and find out whether the vicar had yet made the appointment with Reggie.

"If you go to the study, would you please knock," said Angela. "It's his work-place and not the living-room of the house. Only it costs too much to heat the big room in winters so my father always gets invaded."

"I quite understand," said Clive, quick to take offence at her tone of voice. "I haven't always lived in luxury myself, you know. Mother and I had a basement room in Camden Town before she met Reggie."

"I'm sorry," said Angela. "I'd forgotten. You mentioned it when we were talking to him yesterday. How did your mother and Reggie meet, by the way? I've been wondering quite a lot about that."

Clive laughed shortly. "I expect you have. Most people do. She was going out cleaning houses for an agency. It's a favourite recourse of out-of-work actors and actresses. They sent her one day to Reggie's place in Hampstead. He'd only recently finished one of his wife-changes. Jill's mother had been disposed of by tormenting her so much that she ran away and he then had her for desertion and didn't have to pay a penny, and Reggie had got hold of some wretched little suburban glamour-girl and was putting her though the same process. That one didn't last long. She was sexually incompatible, I believe, but she had wealthy parents and a nice little pad to go back to when she couldn't stick him any longer. Unlike Jill's mother, who drank and drugged and fell to pieces."

"But your own mother?" prompted Angela gently.

"Oh, he took a fancy to her. You'd hardly believe it, but in fact she used to be very lively and attractive. She was installed as resident domestic help and I was tolerated as long as I kept to the servants' quarters. When the current wife was removed, he married my mother. It lasted quite a long time—longer than the other two. I believe he wanted a son and thought it might work this time. You see, Mother had already had me."

They were both silent for a moment and then, with great trepidation, Angela asked the question that had been nagging at her more and more remorselessly.

"About your own father, Clive. Did your mother ever talk about him?"

"Hardly at all. I gather they'd met in the theatre when they were both touring in rep. I've never been shown any photograph or anything. I've just never been told anything."

"Did you get the impression that she felt bitter towards him?"

"No. Not really. If anything I think perhaps she was the one who was feeling guilty. As if in some way she had done the dirty on him. I can't explain how I got this idea. Nothing was ever said, but one sort of gets impressions. You know."

"I know," said Angela softly.

"But she did say once that she would tell me the truth one day, but that it might not be until after she was dead, and so I can't help thinking—I can't help thinking—"

His voice failed. Angela finished the sentence for him.

"You can't help thinking," she said, "that the truth was in the letter that Reginald has stolen from you."

Clive nodded. They stared at each other, seated at either side of the big wooden table in the old-fashioned but cosy vicarage kitchen. And then suddenly, as if both sides had produced electric currents that had met in the centre, there was a flash of something between them, and they both shivered and did not know why.

7

"I'm afraid Mr. Myrtle is not here, Vicar," said Felicity in her sweetest tones over the telephone. "He had to go to London this afternoon and he won't be back till late. Probably *very* late."

She managed to convey the idea that insignificant provincial clergymen could have no conception of the hectic life led by world-famous authors.

"It will have to be tomorrow, then," said Nevil, quite unmoved. "Which do you think he would prefer? To come to me? Or that I should come to the Old Manor?"

"Is Clive still with you?" asked Felicity, changing her tone in the face of this absence of reaction and speaking quite unaffectedly.

"Yes, but he has promised to keep out of the way when I speak to Mr. Myrtle, wherever the interview takes place. I don't know how far one can rely on this promise, but I think it quite likely that I shall be more successful in keeping him out of my study than Mr. Myrtle would be at keeping him out of his."

"Yes, I think you would be," agreed Felicity. "Reggie is absolutely hopeless with Clive. Makes him worse, in fact. What time would suit you? Eleven o'clock?"

"Eleven o'clock tomorrow morning will suit me very
well. I will expect Mr. Myrtle then. Good night."

Nevil rang off with the feeling that this call had been
expected, and that if it had not been made, Felicity
Westbrook would have got in touch with him herself. He sat
thinking for a few minutes and then went to the kitchen to
tell Angela and Clive what had been managed. There was a
sense of great tension in the kitchen: Nevil gave no sign of
being aware of it.

"I shall be going to bed shortly," he said. "If you want
radio or television or anything, don't hesitate to use the
study. You won't disturb me. I'm not going to sleep just
yet. I simply want to be alone to think things over."

And he nodded and smiled at them both and left the
room.

"There's something about your father," said Clive, "that
makes me feel he might even get the better of Reggie. I
really will keep out of the way tomorrow. Honestly."

Angela tried to respond, but found that it was peculiarly
distasteful to her to discuss her father with Clive. She made
the excuse that she was very tired herself. "We've not been
sleeping all day, like you," she said, forcing a smile, and
she begged Clive to do what he liked, borrow books or
records, or take the spare key from the hall table if he
wanted to go out.

It was with a feeling of great relief that she closed her
own bedroom door behind her, selected a story by Charlotte
M. Yonge from the shelf containing her favourite Victorian
classics, and settled down to read. But tonight the magic
failed to work; she could not lose herself in the quaint charm
of a bygone age. She closed the book and glanced at the
picture of her parents. Usually she found it comforting
when she felt worried or uncertain. Here were the roots of
her life, one of them now withered, but still something from
which she herself could grow. But tonight she could not
bear to look at it. She got into bed and pulled the covers
close up round her head as she had done when she was a

frightened child. Sleep came at last, and with it a nightmare of struggling through quicksands towards a tiny flickering light that any moment might go out. She awoke sweating and still hearing her own desperate scream.

"That chair is the most comfortable, Mr. Myrtle," said Nevil. "Angela will be bringing us some coffee in a moment."

"Thanks," said Reginald.

If Reginald was capable of looking ill at ease, then he did so at this moment. Angela's arrival with the tray, however, restored him to his usual complacency.

"Charming girl, your daughter," he said after Angela had departed. "Most unusual colouring of eyes but most effective."

"We have met, I believe," said Nevil coolly, "to discuss the letter that your late wife wrote to your stepson."

"Ah yes, but there are a lot of ramifications, aren't there? Incidentally, I did not purloin the letter. I left it on the table in the hall for Clive and it disappeared. I shall be investigating the possibility of its having been removed by a member of my household."

He got up and wandered over to the bookshelves. "Aristotle—um—Saint Augustine—um—Thomas Aquinas. Well, well. All very scholarly and appropriate. A most convincing setting. And the man to fit the role. You were an actor before you took orders, weren't you, Mr. Grey?"

Reginald returned to his chair and picked up his coffee cup.

"Yes," replied Nevil. "There is no secret about it. Anyone who cares to do so may read the summary of my career in any of the Church directories."

"Might have been quite a distinguished career," said Reginald. "Pity you gave it up."

Nevil made no reply. Reginald put down his coffee cup, picked up the copy of *The Times* that lay on the side table and pretended to glance at it, while saying casually: "Must feel strange, after all these years, to have all your family under one roof."

Nevil's steadily watchful expression did not change, but he sat more rigidly motionless than ever.

"Bit awkward, though, with the young people themselves not knowing," continued Reginald in a conversational manner. "I'd be a little worried about it if I were you."

"Mr. Myrtle," said Nevil in the same quiet tones that he had used throughout, "I am not a rich man. Anyone who cares to make enquiries may easily discover the amount of my stipend. You can hardly be intending to ask me for money. What is it that you want?"

Reginald got up and walked over to the window and looked out. When he turned round again his face appeared distorted as if he were fighting with toothache.

"I want your son and Maureen's," he cried. "But not as yours. As mine. As my own. And I can't have it. You wouldn't understand that, would you, Nevil Grey? You wouldn't understand that we miserable sinners have our feelings too. My father was a parish priest like you. Only I've never put that in the reference books. I've kept it secret. I want to forget him. He hated me. He never wanted me born. He thought sex was sin and children the work of the devil. He made my life a hell. But I didn't want to hand it on—I didn't want a son so that I could torture him as I had been tortured—I wanted a son to make it up to—I wanted a son to be proud of—I wanted—I wanted—"

Reginald broke off and looked out of the window again. Nevil remained seated in the straight chair at the open bureau: he was white and still as a marble statue. When Reginald turned round his face and voice were under better control.

"I hate you, Nevil Grey," he said. "You've got the only thing I ever really longed for and you don't even care. You asked what I want. I want you to suffer. I shall find a way, never fear. Every man has his weakness. Even you. I shall find it."

He moved quickly to the door, paused there, and said with a return to something approaching his normal manner: "Not a very pretty thing to do, is it, to desert a woman when you find she's going to have your child. Not the sort of thing one expects from a guardian of morals and a model of virtue."

Nevil's lips moved at last. "When Maureen and I parted company," he said in a low voice, "I did not know that Clive was already conceived. I did not know that he was my son until a few months ago, but of course I can hardly expect you to believe that."

"Oh, I believe you all right," said Reginald with a sneer. "The question is—will anyone else believe it?"

"May I remind you," replied the vicar, "of your own remark to Clive? There is such a thing as the law of slander."

"That won't wash, you know," retorted Reginald. "You can't head me off by trying any funny business about that letter of Maureen's. No one is ever going to be able to prove that I have ever seen it. No one will ever be able to prove that she didn't tell me about Clive before she died. And in any case we're not dealing in facts. We're dealing in gossip and innuendo, aren't we?—things against which the law is powerless."

"I see," murmured Nevil. "And when is this programme of vilification scheduled to begin?"

The vicar's calm and faintly mocking manner infuriated Reginald, who could not guess what turmoil it concealed. He grasped the door handle, grimaced again, and began to swear at Nevil. Then suddenly he broke off, pulled open the study door and left it standing open as he rushed out of the room. A moment later the front door slammed behind him.

Nevil sat motionless for some time. He had been prepared for something like this, but he had not quite been prepared for the shock of feeling himself the object of another man's naked hatred, nor had he expected to have to struggle with his own feelings of pity for that very man.

After a while he rubbed a hand over his eyes and then took out the old photograph from the little drawer, and laid it in front of him. It showed a smiling, dark-eyed girl dressed in the costume of Shakespeare's Viola. He stared at it, smoothed out the crumpled corner, and slowly shook his head. Why did you have to do it this way, Maureen, he murmured; why did you take such a risk? If you wanted Clive to know, why didn't you let me tell him myself?

He got up and moved restlessly about the room.

What is Reginald going to do? Was that a serious threat? Always wanted a son—poor man, poor man. It explains a lot. And hating his father—a parish priest like myself. Oh yes, it all fits in. Could Maureen have wanted him to steal the letter and suffer from it as he must have suffered? No, that is too fantastic. Nobody could know what would become of it. She meant it only for Clive. She must have thought the news would come better from her words than from mine. But I wish she had told me she was doing it. I might have prevented this. And now . . . and now . . .

With a great effort Nevil managed to get his thoughts into focus.

The main thing now, he said to himself, was to go to Angela. She would have heard the front door shut and be very anxious. But what to tell her, he wondered as he made his way along to the kitchen carrying the tray with the coffee cups. The truth? She would have to be told soon, but not just now. He could not stand anything more just now. A lie—and it would be the first direct lie he had ever told her—would have to be invented if necessary, just to tide him over till he had summoned up the strength to leap the next hurdle.

Angela was seated at the kitchen table with the portable typewriter and various piles of paper in front of her. But there was no paper in the machine and her hands were idle in her lap. She was staring out of the window and from the expression on her face it was plain that her thoughts were not happy ones.

"That was short and sweet," she said, looking round as Nevil came in.

"You can drop the second adjective," he replied.

"What did he say?"

"He said at first that he had left Clive's letter on the hall table and that somebody else in the household must have removed it, and then later on he said that it could never be proved that he had opened and read it."

"I don't believe he hasn't read it," said Angela.

"Neither do I."

There was a short silence.

"So you didn't get much change out of Reggie?" asked Angela, shifting the papers on the table about in an aimless fashion.

"Not much change." Nevil moved over to the sink and washed up the coffee cups, his back towards Angela.

"Was he very unpleasant?" she asked.

"He tried to blackmail me," said Nevil, still busy with the cups.

"Blackmail! Reginald Myrtle! On your income! That's a joke."

"Yes. Very amusing," said Nevil reaching for a tea-towel.

"Anyway, what could there be to blackmail you about," said Angela more as a statement than as a question.

"Oh, there are one or two items in my murky past," replied her father with a ghastly attempt at humour. "Not particularly interesting or serious. I'll tell you later. Just at this moment I feel very much in need of a lowering of the emotional temperature." He walked over to the door. "Where's Clive?" he asked, looked straight at Angela for the first time since he had come into the room. "I've not seen him at all this morning. He's certainly kept his promise to stay out of the way."

"He got up early and went out before you came back from the eight o'clock service," said Angela in an uninterested manner. "He wanted to see Jill and apologize for

mentioning her mother in public the other day. There seems
to be some sort of love-hate relationship between those two.
Love of nobody, hatred of Reginald and of practically
everybody else might be a better way of describing it."

"Then he went to the Old Manor?" Nevil made his voice
as cool and casual as Angela's own.

"No. He phoned there, and Mrs. Westbrook said Jill had
caught an early train to London. Clive thought he might find
her with that couple who came to the funeral. Apparently
she takes refuge with them from time to time."

"Did he say when he'd be back?"

"Not a word. Why? D'you want to see him?"

Nevil shook his head. "Not particularly. But it might be
convenient to know."

"Your guess is as good as mine," said Angela. "Probably
better."

She wound a piece of paper into the machine and typed a
few words at random. Nevil left the room. As soon as he
had gone Angela tore out the paper, crumpled it up and
flung it violently across the room, and then rested her head
on her arms and sobbed, dry-eyed.

Nevil returned to the study and made some telephone
calls. There were two committee meetings he was supposed
to attend that day and he could not face them. When he had
finished he put on his overcoat, for the heating in the church
was not kept full on during the week and he had no wish to
escape his dilemma by deliberately trying to make himself
ill, and let himself quietly out of the house.

The clouds had parted and given way to watery sunshine,
and Nevil paused near the lych-gate, as he often did, to
admire the beautiful setting of the ancient church, with the
clear line of the hills to one side, and to the other, the
latticework of bare trees against the pale blue sky. He went
in through the Norman archway, looked around and saw
that there were no visitors in the building at the moment,
and seated himself on one of the pews at the rear. He raised
his arm and laid it lightly along the back of the pew, crossed

one leg over the other, and stared at the rich reds and blues of the famous east window.

Every man has his weakness, he murmured. Thank you, Reginald, for giving me that text. I will go on from there. My greatest weakness is that I love my neighbour more than I love my god, but the Gospel says that it is the same thing— "inasmuch as ye did it unto the least of these my brethren, ye did it unto me." But I do put too much value on a scrupulous regard for people's feelings, and this can lead to greater cruelty than might otherwise have been. If only I had not promised Maureen that I would never tell Clive . . . if only I had not been so careful not to notice the addresses on the letters she wrote . . . if only . . . if only . . .

But these are vain regrets, and Reginald will not know of this weakness of mine. It will be through the more obvious weakness that he will attack if he is going to. What I love most, what everyone can see that I love most.

Angela.

I would gladly die to save her from hurt. But would I kill to save her? That is the question. She will be hurt—there's no help for that. But how much? I believe I can comfort her private grief; but can I console her in my public disgrace? That is the other question. And even if Reginald were out of the way, there are other people who might still want to harm me. Clive himself for one. He will not love me when he learns the truth.

Nevil smiled bitterly. Am I to contrive a massacre? How? With the wine for the communion service? That would be dramatic indeed. In true Borgia style. Nevertheless it is an idea . . . Reginald has had more than one serious heart attack. If he has another and believes himself to be in danger of dying . . . he is religious in a superstitious way . . . he hates me but he would want a priest . . . Ronnie will soon be back, and Ronnie is very young and inexperienced . . . I wonder . . . I wonder . . .

The vicar of St. Mark's remained for a long time leaning

against the back of the pew in the relaxed and elegant pose of the hero of a drawing-room comedy, while his thoughts ran on. Then he slid to his knees. His trained memory had learnt and retained with ease all the commonly used prayers of the Church, but at this moment they had all emptied from his mind. All except one sentence: "Lead us not into temptation," and he repeated this sentence over and over again.

After a while he got up and stood staring at the glories of the east window as a sudden shaft of sunlight caught the central panel. I love this church, he thought, and I hope whoever follows me will take good care of it. And then he had a strange vision, as if he were outside his own body, seeing it in two different places at the same time. He saw himself at the altar blessing the bread and the wine; and he saw himself standing at the back of the church, a tall figure with greying hair and a thin lined face wearing a faintly ironic smile: a visitor to the village moved by the beauty of the church, a lawyer or politician or even an actor, perhaps.

The figures came together again as Nevil stepped out into the aisle. Perhaps there would be that way out for him. People had left the ministry under a cloud before now and built up a new life for themselves and those who loved them. It wouldn't be the same but it would be a life of sorts. The whole thing really depended on Angela's reactions when she learnt the truth. He was beginning to gather up the strength to tell her, but he would walk on the Downs for a little while before going back. She would not expect him just yet in any case; she didn't know he had cancelled his meetings, so she would not be anxious about him.

— 8 —

Angela raised her head from her arms, turned over some manuscript pages, and found the place where she had left off her typing of the thesis on fiscal policy. Then she put some more paper into the typewriter, but instead of settling down to work, she found herself copying out the same sentence over and over again.

"The phrase 'cheap money' is difficult to define in precise terms."

She typed it without thinking, but deriving some relief from the slight occupation of mind and hand, as if it were a sort of magic incantation, while all the time she was struggling in the quicksands of her nightmare, which seemed now to have taken over her waking life. Her mother, to whom Angela had never been very close, had once said to her in a rare burst of feeling: "You must try not to idolize your father, my child. You'll have a nasty shock one day, or else you will spend the rest of your life rejecting prospective husbands because they don't measure up to your ideal."

It looked, thought Angela, tearing out yet another sheet of futile typescript, as if both prophecies were going to come true. That the shock was coming she had no doubt;

she was already feeling its effect, and probably imagining the facts to be far worse than they really were. And as for rejecting prospective husbands, why, she had been doing that ever since she was sixteen, without really being able to give a reason, except that the young men all seemed to be so dull and so lacking in character. That was why Gary had attracted her so much: he had poise and maturity and self-control—or rather, she had believed that he had, and when he turned out to be weak and cowardly the disillusion had been very great. And now if her father was going to let her down too . . .

What had happened during that interview with Reggie? If her father was in great trouble then why hadn't he told her so that they could face it together? Blackmail, he had said. The idea was ludicrous. Or was it? Even the very best of people had sometimes been discovered to be leading double lives.

"Oh, this is perfectly ridiculous!" exclaimed Angela aloud. She got up from the table and shook herself impatiently. "As if Dad would be doing a Jekyll and Hyde act! I'm jealous of Clive, that's all. It's very silly of me but we all get childish sometimes. Damn Clive! Let's forget him and try to get back to normal."

Very deliberately she tidied up her papers and put away the typewriter. Then she wandered into the big front room of the vicarage. It was at about the same moment as Nevil was standing admiring the shaft of sunlight breaking on the east window in the church. The same burst of sun hit the windows of the vicarage, and brought a touch of warmth even into the great unheated room. Angela stood at the window, looking out across the garden to the front gate, feasting her eyes and mind on the safe, familiar things. The crocuses under the apple tree were showing a glimmer of yellow; the forsythia already had a couple of branches in bloom. It would be just right for decorating the church at Easter, she thought.

A young woman pushing a pram passed by the open gate,

looked up and saw Angela at the window, and smiled and waved. Jennifer Prescott. She'd had a bad dose of 'flu. Dad would be pleased to know she was up and about again. And it would be one less call to make. He spent too much time, in Angela's opinion, visiting sick people, both in Southdene and at the hospital. They were always asking him to come, including many people in the new industrial estate who never came to church. They swore he did them more good than the doctor. Not by doing or saying anything in particular; just by listening unmoved to all their fears and doubts, and by silently conveying a great sense of reassurance and peace, a feeling that there was no pain or grief that would not come to an end; that all would be well.

And it's probably just all acting, thought Angela bitterly; I don't believe he really believes in anything. It's a great big con trick, that's all. And I've been taken in too. he ought to have kept the other side of the footlights, where it wouldn't have mattered. She gripped the window-sill and stared out at the garden, trying to lose herself in the sight of the sunlight on the bushes, the glimpse of the road and the corner of the village green. And then suddenly she stiffened. Another figure had appeared in the open gateway, and it was turning and coming in towards the house. For a split second she thought it was her father returning: the man was of the same height and build, and with the sun behind him, showed up only in silhouette. But her father would be wearing a coat, not jeans and an anorak, and Angela drew hastily back from the window when she realized that it was Clive.

I don't want to see him, was her instant reaction; I can't bear to talk about his problems just now. But he has got a key, was her next thought; he's staying here; I can't stop him coming in.

She moved into the hall, wondering where to find the strength to welcome him as he surely deserved. He'll want to know what happened with Reginald . . . what shall I say? . . . how can I hide my own fears?

She heard the sound of footsteps coming very near and braced herself for the ordeal. But the door did not open. Instead, the flap of the letter-box came up and an envelope dropped through into the wire basket below. Am I having hallucinations, was Angela's first fleeting thought: did I really see Clive?

She rushed to the door and flung it open. Clive was a few feet away from her, walking down the path towards the gate.

"Clive!" she shouted as she ran after him.

He stopped and turned to face her.

"Clive!" she caught his arm. "Whatever's the matter?"

He shook her off. "Do you really need to ask?"

"Yes, I do! What do you think you're doing? Why don't you come in? What's that envelope you've just put through the letter-box?"

"That envelope contains a letter. The famous letter. Or rather, a copy of it. It also contains a covering note. Written by me to—" He paused. "To our father," he added.

"To our—!" Angela broke off and breathed quickly. She had gone very pale.

"So you didn't know," said Clive, studying her closely and speaking in a slightly kinder tone. "Move up a grade, Angy. At least you're not the hypocrite I took you for."

He made as if to walk on. Angela caught his arm again and hastily dropped it when he pulled away, but remained blocking his path.

"You can't go like that!" she cried. "You've got to tell me—you've got to explain yourself."

Clive appeared to think for a moment or two. "Okay," he said at last. "I suppose you've a right to hear. But I mustn't be too long. Jill's waiting for me over by the duckpond and then we're going home to tackle her own paternal parent. Though I will say this for Reggie, bastard though he is, at least he's not a hypocrite."

"How did you learn—what you've just said?" asked

Angela. She was still breathing very quickly but her voice was steady.

"Jill got hold of the letter. Bright girl, Jill. She found Felicity snooping around Reggie's study at night and decided to play her along a bit and pretend to help. Jill found the letter all right, but didn't let on to Felicity. It was slipped into one of the envelopes in a new box that hadn't yet been started. Anyone would think it was simply an untouched box of envelopes, but Jill thought of it because Reggie once wrote a story using that as a hiding-place and Jill remembered it. Felicity was hunting somewhere else, and didn't see, and when they'd both given up and Felicity had gone back to bed, Jill came down again and copied the letter and put the original back where it had been before so that Reggie would think nobody had seen it. We've made another copy for me and we're going to have some fun with Reggie and Felicity this evening. We've got it all planned out—how to make them sweat not knowing how much we know. I reckon I'll get at the truth that way. But meanwhile I told Jill I'd got this little errand to do first. I wanted to deliver my own message personally to our most reverend father. Get the picture? Must rush now. Sorry to deprive you so soon of your long-lost brother, Angy."

He looked at her with the same mixture of pity and irritation with which she had once looked at him.

"I'd go away if I were you, Angy," he said. "Clear out and have a bit of fun. It's not worth crying over. Nobody's worth it. Good luck. So long."

And he raised his arm and patted her shoulder in a somewhat embarrassed manner before hurrying off to join Jill.

Angela returned to the house like a sleepwalker. The telephone was ringing as she came into the hall, and she answered it and made a note of the message and left it on her father's desk. Almost immediately the phone rang again, and she wrote out another message. Then she sat down at the desk and instantly got to her feet again. Shall I go away, she asked herself, knowing the answer only too well. Clive is lucky, she thought enviously, he's got a way out, he can shake things off. Curiosity arose about the letter from Maureen Myrtle. God knows it's caused enough trouble, said Angela to herself; and here it is. I might as well read it.

The envelope was addressed to the vicar in a hand that was strange to Angela. Jill Myrtle, I suppose, she thought: she and Clive had obviously discussed the whole thing. And the notion made her shudder, as if she could already see headlines in the Sunday papers— "Vicar's Guilty Secret."

But it's they who are the hypocrites, she exclaimed aloud; who the hell really cares about an illegitimate son? When has Dad ever pretended to be anything other than he is?

But he has pretended, she immediately replied to herself. He has been pretending to me all these years. He's kept this from me, he hasn't confided in me. And the full hurt of this burst over her, and she ripped open the sealed envelope, crying: "I don't care if it's opening other people's letters—I don't care! He's forfeited the right to have me care."

There were several sheets of paper within the foolscap envelope. The top one, containing Clive's message, Angela put to the bottom to read at the end. Maureen Myrtle's letter did not take very long to read. Jill's handwriting was clear but rather sprawling: a neater hand would have contained the whole message in fewer pages.

My darling boy [it began], forgive me the unhappiness I have brought you and forgive me for telling you in this way. I promised you I would tell you one day who your father was, and now that I am no longer there to protect you I want you to turn to him. We loved each other long ago. Very much. He has never harmed me, you must believe that. It has all been my fault. Please forgive me, and please let him help you now. He is a good man and can give you good advice.

There followed a few sentences naming Nevil and mentioning some incidents of his early career of which Angela had never heard. The last page of Jill's handwriting contained mostly renewed expressions of contrition and love and concern for Clive, and at the very bottom was written: "You had better leave the Old Manor at once and keep away from your stepfather. Your father will advise you. And for God's sake don't let your stepfather know what I have written here because . . ."

Angela turned the page. There was nothing more. She was back at Clive's covering note again. She checked through the pages in Jill's handwriting to see if one had got out of order, but found nothing to follow on to this last half sentence. Damn the girl, she thought; why couldn't she do the job properly while she was about it. Perhaps Clive's covering note would explain. Angela picked this up, and as she read it she became first scarlet and then even more pale than before.

Dear Father [it ran], here is a copy of the letter from beyond the grave, for information only. Do you think it was quite fair to loose my glamorous sister at me? I thought parsons were supposed to be rather fussy about that sort of thing. However, there is no harm done. Not on my side, at least. Thank you for all the trouble you have taken on my behalf. It must have been very worrying to you, in your position. Just too bad. But don't trouble any more. I reckon I can look after myself very well, thank you. So I will therefore sign off, for the first and the last time, as your most disobedient and unaffectionate disrespectful and very ungrateful son, Clive Bradley.

Angela dropped all the sheets of paper on to her father's desk, to which she had returned while she read the letter. I suppose, she thought in a dull way, it is understandable that Clive should take it like that. She glanced at Clive's

message again and imagined what her father would feel like
when he read it.

Shall I spare him that, she asked herself: easy enough to
destroy that page.

And then she got to her feet and banged her fist down on
the little pile of paper that lay on the desk. No, no, no! Why
should I spare him anything?

She ran to the door of the study. At the same moment the
front door was pushed open. Nevil stood still just in front of
it when he saw Angela.

"I think I'm going to be sick," she cried, and ran
upstairs.

Some time later she came down again, clasping in both
hands the photograph that always stood on her bedside
table. When she reached the open study door she turned it
round and held the picture out to Nevil, who was sitting at
the desk, staring at nothing.

"Will you please—tell me truthfully," said Angela,
speaking in little tight clipped phrases, "whether this is a
picture—of both my parents—or of neither of them— or of
either—and if so, of which one?"

Lying among the papers on the desk was a paperback
copy of a new translation of the Bible that Nevil had been
sent to review. He stood up and reached out to rest his hand
on this as he replied: "That photograph is a picture of both
your parents. That is the truth. I swear it."

Angela turned the photograph round, clutched it to her
again, closed her eyes, and swayed a little. "I think I can
stand it then," she muttered, and then added, in a more
natural voice: "Hold on—I'm going to be sick again."

When she returned to the room, without the photograph,
she was still deathly white and her hair, usually so uncon-
trollably full of life, was hanging damply round her face.
But when she spoke it was in her normal manner.

"Well, that's all over, Dad. Frightfuly melodramatic,
wasn't it? Do you think I've missed my vocation? At least
I know now why Clive has inherited such a talent for

making scenes. Though of course his mother was an actress too, and actually you don't create scenes, do you?"

Nevil shook his head. He could not speak.

"No, you don't need to," went on Angela. "They just seem to happen round you, and I know you don't enjoy them. Sorry about this one. It won't occur again, I promise. I think tea is the next thing on the agenda, don't you, and after that we'd better get down to a brain-storming session on the subject of what to do about Reggie's blackmail. Come on." She took her father's arm and pulled him unresisting towards the most comfortable armchair. "Lean back and shut your eyes. I shan't be long."

9

About an hour later Nevil said: "Well, that is the truth and nothing but the truth, but I may have omitted some details that you would like to know about. Cross-examine me as much as you like."

Angela was silent for a little while, digesting the story she had just listened to. The vicarage study was warm and comfortable. The century-old shutters and the heavy old curtains muffled the storm that had followed the afternoon's sunshine, and the log fire was burning well. Don't let anyone in the parish choose this moment to turn up with their problems, prayed Angela: let's have just a little longer to ourselves.

"You and Maureen loved each other," she said at last. "You both knew all about the unsettled sort of lives that actors have to lead. But there have been plenty of successful marriage partnerships in the theatre. You wanted to marry her. Why wouldn't she marry you? Did she have conscientious objections to marriage? And if so, then why did she marry Reggie?"

"She didn't object to marriage in general," replied Nevil. "Only to marrying me."

"But why, *why!*" exclaimed Angela. "It doesn't make

sense. She loved you. She probably never stopped loving you," she added bitterly.

Nevil rubbed a hand across his eyes. "I think that was the trouble," he said after a while. "I don't know whether she was afraid that she couldn't trust me to be faithful to her, or what it was, but she said—" and in spite of all his self-control there was no disguising the note of deep, long-remembered pain—"she said I was too cruel a man to love for a lifetime and she would rather try to keep a little of herself free from me. It upset me badly. I used to get very upset in those days. I couldn't understand what she meant. Can you?"

Angela stared at her father. "Yes, I believe I can," she said at last. "Yes, I can understand what she meant."

Nevil looked at her unhappily. "Am I cruel, Angy?"

"Never intentionally. Is the lamp cruel because the moth loves the light and bruises its wings in trying to reach it? No. Of course you are never unkind. You are absolutely overflowing with Christian charity. You're just unapproachable, that's all. Other people's emotions beat against you in vain. Poor Maureen. What it must have cost her to tear herself away! And then to find she was going to have a child—and I suppose she was too proud to tell you. And in any case you'd by that time taken up with one of your old loves . . . oh, my God! Poor Mother!"

Tears started into Angela's eyes and she brushed them aside impatiently. "So you married Mother on the rebound," she said lightly. "As a sort of second best. And I suppose it was brooding over Maureen's words that eventually sent you into the Church—a sort of working out the feeling of guilt. And poor Mother had to give up her lovely home. But she adored you too and she was very emotional and was for ever beating her wings without result. And then myself—" She paused for a moment before adding, even more casually: "You know, Dad, for a good Christian who loves all the world you've created a surprising amount of havoc among those who have loved you."

Nevil recoiled as though someone had struck him in the face. The telephone rang and he turned to pick up the receiver.

"It doesn't matter a bit," he said to the caller after listening in silence for a while. "I shall be very happy to christen your son. Would you care to call and discuss the details? Or would you rather I came round to you?"

"That's the new people who've bought the cottage next to Martha's Pantry," he said as he replaced the receiver. "Worried because the boy is six years old and they're only just got round to having him christened. Some people don't find me so very unapproachable," he added with a very rare note of self-defensiveness creeping into his voice.

Angela laughed. "Of course not, you idiot. You're super with everybody except those closest to you. Perhaps you are in the right job, after all. Cheer up. I dare say I'll marry some harmless young nitwit one of these days and produce a brace of grandchildren for you before you die. You'd like that, wouldn't you?"

Nevil admitted that he would.

Angela nodded. "Yes. It stirred things up, didn't it, Maureen telling you about Clive. Reggie's not the only one who badly wanted a son."

The vicar shrugged. "One has some strange primitive instincts about it," he said. "I must say I could not help feeling sorry for Reginald in spite of everything."

"I can! Loving my enemies is not my strong point," cried Angela warmly. "And I reckon you can spare your pity for better objects than Reggie. I wish you'd called me in when he was twisting the knife in the wound and let me have a go at him!" She thought for a moment. "Never mind. You're a tough old devil and you'll come through this business all right. We both will. How do we shut up Reggie, that's the point."

"Short of murdering him," said Nevil lightly, "I really don't know."

"I'm prepared to do that if necessary," said Angela in

similar tones, "but I'd rather not have to. How much harm can he do us, Dad?"

"Our unfortunate society," said Nevil, "seldom has the pleasure of watching a man's fall from virtue because there are so few people left who have any pretensions to virtue in the first place. Scandals about politicians have become a bore, and even the indiscretions of royalty don't provide the thrill that they did twenty years ago. I should think that a story about a priest fallen from grace would still make fairly interesting reading, however, if handled by someone skilled in the art of character-assassination."

"But it isn't a crime to have an illegitimate child," cried Angela. "And you weren't even a clergyman at the time. Nobody who knows you will give a damn when they hear the story."

"Ah, but they won't hear the story I've just told you. They will hear Reggie's, and that will be a very different matter. He hinted at it when he was here. The story will go that I abandoned a girl when I learned she was expecting my child. It's no good, my dear. We have to face it. Reginald hates me, and if he really chooses to pillory me he has the means to do it. I only wish you did not have to join me there. Perhaps you ought to go away for a while."

"We might both go away," said Angela, "and leave Ronnie to hold the fort. He'll be back tomorrow."

Nevil shook his head. "You don't really want me to run away, do you?"

"That's out then," said Angela. "How can we buy Reginald off? Money's no good. What else can we offer that he might want?"

Suddenly she began to laugh. "He is quite taken with me, you know. Perhaps I'd better go and offer myself! Like Shakespeare's Isabella—sacrificing her virginity in order to save her brother's life. Except that it wouldn't be a sacrifice of virginity in my case."

"I never supposed that it would," snapped her father. "Have I ever interfered with your casual affairs?"

"Never," returned Angela with a similar burst of irritation. "You've been too damned perfect about that too. That's what first made me feel suspicious about Clive, by the way. I know you dread my getting married, but you don't usually bring it out into the open like that. Anyway, this sacrificial lamb business is a non-starter too because it would only hold Reggie for a little while, if at all. Unless," and she became very thoughtful, "unless I could make him believe he was getting his own back on you by seducing your daughter."

She got up and began to rove about the room, talking excitedly. "You don't know, Dad, that really is an idea. I'm quite serious about it. Reggie hates you and wants to wallop you. Doing it through me might really appeal to him."

"It might," said Nevil slowly. "In fact I have no doubt that it would."

He got to his feet to throw more logs on the fire, and then straightened up and said with great firmness: "But I won't have it. You obviously fancy yourself acting the role of dishonoured daughter and no doubt you could make a success of it. Go and sleep with Reggie if you want to, but not on my account nor with any motive other than experimentation or the pursuit of pleasure. Damn it, Angela, I've already got a reputation for being a broad-minded parson and what my reputation will be like when Reggie's finished with it God alone knows, but this really is the limit. I won't have it and that's final."

"Then there's nothing left but to blackmail him into leaving you alone," said Angela.

"How?" asked Nevil, sitting down wearily again after the little outburst of feeling.

"Maureen's death, of course. We've rather lost sight of that, haven't we, in all our other upsets. It's a pity we've also lost Clive as an ally, but we'll just have to plug away on our own, since even if Clive comes round, we can't rely on him. I don't know whether you noticed that Maureen's letter was not complete. I thought at first that Jill or Clive had left a page out of the envelope by mistake, but I'm wondering now whether it wasn't deliberately omitted. I'll get the letter. Look. You see what I mean?"

They pored over the unfinished sentence together: "And for God's sake don't let your stepfather know what I have written here because . . ."

"Very interesting," said Nevil.

"Very interesting indeed," corrected Angela.

"It's a pity," said Clive as he and Jill walked along the village street in the direction of the dual carriageway, "that you didn't get the whole of my mother's letter."

"It's a pity it wasn't you who had to take the risk," retorted Jill, flaring up as was her habit at the least hint of criticism. "I suppose if Father had caught you snooping round his study you'd have given him a sock on the jaw. Well, it so happens that I can't do that, and it makes quite a bit of difference."

"Cool it, cool it, child," said Clive, taking her arm. "You've done a grand job. I only said it was a pity you thought you heard your father coming before you'd finished the copying."

"I didn't only think I heard. I did hear. I was lucky to get everything back to square one and be in the kitchen putting on the kettle when he appeared in the corridor. He looked like hell and practically collapsed at my feet. I swear Felicity had doped him."

"Couldn't you go back tonight and get the rest of the letter?" asked Clive. "Or if you're scared to remove it, at least you can see what it says."

"He's taken it away," said Jill. "I looked yesterday evening when he'd gone to London and Felicity was on the phone."

"Hidden somewhere else in the house?"

"Shouldn't think so. He's probably burnt it."

"I don't think Reggie would destroy it just yet. He'd want to keep it to hold over me—and over my old man."

"Then he's probably carrying it around with him," said Jill without much interest. She felt that she had heard quite enough for one day of Clive's reactions to the revelation about who his father was and she didn't want to go through all the convolutions of astonishment and shock and bitterness and anger yet again. It was most unusual for her to listen so patiently to anybody as she had listened to Clive, not to mention copying out the letter again for him and hanging about the village green while he delivered his message to the vicarage. He ought to be grateful to her, she felt, and not nag about the rest of the letter.

"You didn't even get a glimpse of what came next?" asked Clive.

"For the umpteenth time, no, I didn't," cried Jill. "I was just going to turn the page. There was only one more."

"I'd have thought you'd have read it right through before starting to copy it," said Clive.

"Well I didn't," snapped Jill. "And if you're going on like this I shall be sorry I ever told you about it at all."

"Hey! That's rich!" cried Clive. "It was my letter, remember? My mother's letter addressed to me that your father went and stole before I could read it."

"Oh I know," replied Jill, subsiding as quickly as she had flared up. "I'm sorry. It was Father at his meanest and I'm not defending him."

"Pity you didn't take it away to hand on to me as it ought to've been handed in the first place," said Clive, "when you saw it was addressed to me."

They had reached the dual carriageway and were standing waiting for a lull in the seemingly endless stream of traffic so that they could at least get to the central strip of grass.

"I've already explained," said Jill with weary patience, "that when I found that letter I'd no intention of doing you a favour. You'd hit my father in public and you'd said something rather beastly to me. Also in public. I wasn't feeling at all kindly towards you. If you really must know, I hunted for that letter partly because I thought it might help me to get my own back on you and partly because I thought it might give me some sort of hold over Father. I wanted to know what he was up to. And now you know it all. Come on. We can get half across."

She grabbed Clive by the hand and they raced over the road not many yards in front of a heavy lorry. During the wait at the second carriageway she said: "Actually after I'd thought about it that night, I felt you'd been so meanly treated that I was going to show you my copy of the letter in any case, even if you hadn't come along this morning and apologized. Oh hurry up, Clive!"

She grabbed him again and this time there was a screech of brakes and a curse from the driver who had been obliged to slow down to avoid hitting them.

"That bloody road!" cried Jill when they were safely in the steep lane leading up to the Old Manor. "How I loathe having to wait for anything."

"I won't say what I'm thinking," said Clive, putting an arm round her, "because it isn't quite decent, and I mustn't forget that I'm the son of a parson, must I? It's funny, isn't it, that you and I are quite unrelated to each other and yet I feel we're more like brother and sister, whereas my real sister . . ."

His voice trailed away.

"Oh for Christ's sake!" exclaimed Jill. "If she turns you on as much as all that, you'd better go and have a go at her. I don't suppose she'd object. You're not so bad, as men go nowadays. And I don't suppose it really matters so long as there aren't any kids to be born loony or deformed or whatever happens from incestuous unions."

"And you're not so bad, either, Jilly. And I'm not really hankering after Angela. She's very easy to look at and she's a smashing cook and I shouldn't say she was exactly frigid but she's not my type. Too idealistic for my sinful nature. No. You and I will suit each other very well, Jilly, but we've got to have some money. We'd be hopeless at being poor."

"Now you're talking," said Jill, "and about time too. Don't walk so quickly. We don't want to get there till our plan of campaign is worked out."

"Ultimate aim: your father's money when he dies, and if possible get hold of it before then. More immediate objective: stop him marrying Felicity or any other woman upon whom he might beget legal issue. You know, we've set ourselves some task, Jill, considering your father's capacity for collecting and shedding wives. And he's not all that old. He could go on like this for another twenty years."

"He could but I don't think he will. I overheard Dr. Jephcott telling Maureen that Father was going to have to cut down on the smokes and the booze if he wanted his heart to last out the normal life span."

Clive glanced at her curiously. "Would you actually do away with him if you had the chance, Jill?" he asked.

"If he'd just made a will in my favour, and if someone like Felicity came along who looked like making him switch it to theirs, then I'd be very tempted to slip something into his rum nightcap before he had a chance to change his will," said Jill grimly. "Oh well," she added a moment later, "I suppose I wouldn't really. I mean, blood is blood. However bad it is. If you see what I mean."

Clive did not reply.

"Oh Lord. Now I've put my foot in it again," cried Jill. "Look, if you're still brooding over your suspicion that my dad hustled on your mother's death, forget it. There's no point in us getting together if we don't trust each other."

"No point at all," agreed Clive.

"Right. Then the first thing we've got to do is to turn Father against Felicity. And the best way for that is for me to tell him she was snooping in his study after putting dope in his drink. He'll believe me against her. It's a funny thing, but he does believe what I tell him."

"Which in this case happens to be true."

"Right. Then according to how he takes it, I filter out the contents of the letter—as if it was Felicity who had told me.

And then we play it from there. But there's just one thing, Clive."

Jill paused between the gateposts of the Old Manor. The wrought-iron gates were propped open. Reginald's Rover was standing outside the garage door and Felicity's little Fiat was on the gravel. The light was fading; storm clouds were gathering over the distant horizon.

"The whole thing is going to fall to pieces at once if you lose your temper with Father," said Jill. "Just keep your trap shut if you feel your gorge rising and remember the glittering prizes. He's not going to welcome you with open arms, but he'll tolerate you if you keep your cool. I did a bit of spade-work on him yesterday before he went to London and he seemed to be thawing a little. I haven't seen him since, but as far as I know there's been nothing to needle him. He always likes showing off at the Authors' Dinner— that was last night, and this morning he'll have enjoyed himself rubbing the vicar's nose in the dirt. He ought to be in a genial mood. So just you keep your fists to yourself. Right?"

"Right," said Clive with a show of enthusiasm, which in fact he was far from feeling. The reaction against this conspiracy with Jill was beginning to set in. Gratitude to her for getting hold of his mother's letter and for helping him over the first shock of its contents was very strong; under the influence of this, and of his own immediate feeling of bitterness against Nevil, he had scribbled down the first sequence of wounding sentences that came into his head, and showed them to Jill as the note he proposed to write to his newly-discovered father. She had approved it, and after that it was impossible to draw back from this attitude of resentment and toughness and bravado, though in his heart Clive was beginning to regret it even before his encounter with Angela in the vicarage garden. During the ensuing talk with Jill he was regretting it more and more, and the thought of Reginald crowing in triumph over the vicar disgusted him.

Not only that, but he could not, in spite of Jill's insistence, forget his suspicion that Reggie had hastened on his mother's death. And to this was added Clive's own suspicion that Jill, for all her ready explanations, did in fact know perfectly well what was in the missing page of his mother's letter. Of course she had read right through it before starting to copy it out; no human being would have failed to. She knew all right, and was determined to keep it from him. And the reason for this could only be, surely, that Clive's mother had hinted in the end of the letter that Reginald was poisoning her. Thus Clive reasoned; but if this was the case, was Jill keeping quiet about it because of a residue of loyalty and affection for her father, or was she just playing Clive along as she had played Felicity, before eventually going it alone with this hold that she had over Reginald?

Well, he was too deeply involved to draw back now. He would have to keep cool, as Jill had ordered, and keep his thoughts to himself.

10

Felicity had just reached the foot of the stairs when Clive and Jill came into the front hall of the Old Manor. She had been looking both tired and worried as she came down, but her face strained itself into its habitual sweetness when she saw them.

"Hullo, Clive," she said. "Have you decided to come back? Weren't you feeling too comfortable at the vicarage?"

Jill gave Clive quite a vicious kick on the shin as they moved into the drawing-room, and he stifled both a squeal of pain and any hasty retort that might have risen to his lips, before he replied to Felicity.

"I met Jill in London," he said, "and we came back on the same train and got the bus out from Brighton together."

"And then had ever such a nice little walk and talk, I expect," said Felicity.

"Where's Father?" said Jill, ignoring this.

"He's not at all well. I've just been up to see if he wants to come down to dinner," said Felicity.

Jill and Clive exchanged glances.

"What's the matter with him?" asked Jill.

"He came back from the vicarage at lunch-time and said he couldn't be bothered to put the car into the garage—I'll have to do it in a moment," said Felicity in parenthesis, "and he didn't want any lunch but went straight to lie down. He said he was feeling very tense so I gave him a mild tranquillizer."

"I bet you did," murmured Jill under her breath, and Clive asked as politely as he could what Mrs. Westbrook thought had happened at the vicarage to upset Reggie.

"I haven't the slightest idea," replied Felicity, opening her eyes to their widest expanse of innocent-looking blue. "He was to discuss some private business with the vicar, I believe. It wasn't for me to ask what it was."

The hell it wasn't. This time it was Clive who muttered under his breath. Could it possibly be, he thought, that the old man had sent Reggie away with a flea in his ear? The idea caught his fancy, and for a moment or two he wondered whether he could possibly ask Angela, and whether perhaps he had not, after all, forfeited all right to receive a welcome at the vicarage.

"Oh well," said Jill to Felicity, "if Dad isn't fit for dinner and you don't want any, I guess Clive and I had better rummage for ourselves in the kitchen."

"I didn't say I didn't want any," retorted Felicity. "As a matter of fact your father intends to come down. There's some pheasant and smoked salmon and some of that special pâté—it's mostly cold, but rather special, since as a matter of fact your father and I had planned to have a quiet little celebration together this evening. Just a modest little dinner for two here at home."

"I thought your home was North Lane Cottage," said Clive nastily before Jill could stop him. "Not the Old Manor."

"Well, of course it is a little too soon for us actually to get married," said Felicity, plumping up a sofa cushion that didn't really need it. "But I don't think we need to wait very long, and there's no point in being hypocritical about it, is there?"

Clive was about to explain about his mother, but Jill frowned him into silence.

"So you were going to celebrate your engagement to my father this evening, were you?" she said to Felicity in deadpan tones. "I congratulate you. That was quick work. Has he altered his will yet? Or does that wait until after the ceremony?"

"Well really!" exclaimed Felicity, turning round from an unnecessary adjustment of the vases on the mantelpiece. "I don't think it's quite tactful to mention that at this moment, is it," and she glanced at Clive.

"Oh Clive's expecting nothing from Father," said Jill. "It's me I'm talking about. After all, I'm his heir now, and his only near relative, aren't I? He's always said he was going to leave me a packet to make up a bit for—to make up for—" Her defiant manner slipped for a moment and she cleared her throat before she went on. "He promised to leave me his money and I'm bloody well going to make sure I get it. That's all."

Felicity drew in her breath with a little hiss. She looked like a cat tensing up for the pounce.

"So we're out in the open now," she said softly.

"Yes. We're out in the open," replied Jill.

At that moment the door of the drawing-room was flung open and Reginald stood there, taking in the scene.

"Ah, so we have company," he said. "And a nice little cat fight going on, by the sound of it."

He glanced at Clive, who merely nodded. For once he was not entirely sorry to see Reginald and he even, for a very brief moment, had a faint flicker of sympathy for him. Reginald seemed to sense this. Their eyes met in silent comment on the women's behavior and Clive felt that his presence in the house was going to be tolerated, at any rate for the moment.

Reginald advanced into the room. He looked rather bleary about the eyes and his colour was bad but he moved and spoke with his usual assurance.

"Would you mind postponing the baring of teeth and claws," he said to Felicity and Jill, "until we have had dinner? If you wish to return to the fray afterwards I shall be very pleased to assist by laying my bet on Jill. She hasn't your experience, Fizzy, but she's younger and tougher and she'll last out more rounds. But meanwhile such excitements are no aid to the digestion, and mine is already not quite what it ought to be. Come on. Go and get yourselves some plates and glasses, you youngsters, and bring them into the dining-room. There's plenty of food. I do believe we are going to have quite an interesting little party after all."

Reginald's eyes were indeed beginning to light up at the prospect of mischief as he took Felicity's arm and led her with state into the dining-room. She submitted with barely concealed ill-grace and behind their backs Jill made frantic gestures and grimaces at Clive. Just what these were intended to convey, he could not guess, but he grinned back at her reassuringly and held up his thumbs.

In fact Clive was feeling every moment more and more detached from Jill and her schemes. The whole set-up at the Old Manor had become quite unreal to him. Reality lay in a comfortably shabby room with a log-fire burning, and an austere-looking grey-haired man with kind eyes, and a girl with glowing sunset hair. But they are my folks, my own real folks, he kept saying to himself with amazement. I was actually staying there; I could have had it as my home.

The other three were bitching away at each other. Felicity kept protesting that it would do Reggie harm if he ate and drank too much, but at the same time, Clive noted in his strange state of detachment, she kept loading up his plate and filling up his glass. What does she want to do, he asked himself: make Reggie ill so that he becomes completely dependent on her? Reginald when ill was a very different being from Reginald at the top of his form. He became panicky, morbid, and obsessively penitent; and above all, very malleable to the influence of whoever happened to be near.

That must be it, thought Clive, and noticed that Jill too was perfectly aware of what Felicity was doing. She grabbed the bottle that Felicity was holding poised over her father's glass, and filled up her own glass and Clive's with its remaining contents.

"Oh never mind, Dad," she cried with a very unconvincing air of apology. "Why don't you go on to the brandy? It'd be better for your digestion."

Clive smiled to himself. You won't do it that way, my girl, he thought: so much for all your preaching subtlety and self-control to me.

"We'll have another bottle of the burgundy, I think, Fizzy," said Reginald, beaming at Felicity, who hurried away to fetch it, and the very click of her heels on the polished floorboards expressed her triumph.

"Very nice of you, I'm sure," said Reggie, turning to Jill, "to take so much interest in your poor old father's state of health."

Jill relapsed into sullen silence, but she had her chance a little later on, when Reginald remarked casually in his most condescending tones: "Very charming girl, Angela Grey. Pity she should have to waste her talents in a country vicarage. Ought to make a good marriage."

Jill gave Clive a warning look. He had indeed felt a spurt of anger rising and was surprised how easily he had managed to bring it under control even before Jill's glance.

"I don't suppose she stays single for lack of asking," said Jill. And then a moment later she added with a self-conscious little laugh: "Why don't you enter the market yourself, Dad? You need a younger wife this time. It'd buck you up no end."

Felicity made a little splutter into her wine-glass, put it down on the table, and wiped her mouth primly with her napkin.

"It's not a bad idea," said Reggie, "and it would be a delightful revenge on that smug parent of hers."

The other three stared at him and then at each other. Neither Jill nor Felicity felt quite sure how to respond to this, and Clive was continuing to astonish himself by his unprecedented self-control.

"I assume you all know," continued Reggie, "that our reverend friend down at the vicarage is the unacknowledged parent of young Clive here."

He looked keenly at each one in turn: all three stared at their plates and said nothing.

"You do all know. Well, I won't inquire how you came to know. That is perhaps best forgotten. You will be interested to hear, however, that the man does not deny this and that—" Here Reggie broke off and his face, already very red, became more apoplectic than ever. "He had the insufferable cheek to behave as if *I* was the one to be pitied—I—I—presumably for not having the honour to admit to paternity in the case of this worthless young man here."

Reginald looked down the table at Clive. He's getting very drunk, thought Clive. He can still talk all right but he's not in full control of what he's saying.

"Damn his bloody charity!" exclaimed Reggie banging a fist on the table so hard that the glasses rattled. "I'm going to skin that fellow!"

It occurred to Jill that this was a good moment to intervene. "Clive has already started the process, Dad," she said. "He wrote him a real stinger of a letter. We delivered it this afternoon."

And she repeated, with great glee and to her father's evident satisfaction, the gist of the note that Clive had written to Nevil.

"That's great, that's great!" cried Reginald when she had finished. "This calls for another glass. Well done, my boy, well done." He beamed upon Clive with eyes slightly out of focus. "Carry on the good work like that and you'll be remembered in my will. Come on, Fizzy, drink up, girl. You're not forgotten either. Come on, all of you. Lend me your wits. Let's pool our ideas about how to crucify our saintly friend."

It was fortunate for Clive that Reginald was not far off the point of passing out, for he did not think his self-control would have lasted for very much longer. Eventually Reggie got to his feet, instantly fell back into his chair again, said "Damn" quietly, and shut his eyes. Clive helped Felicity and Jill to get him upstairs and then left them to put him to bed, while he hurried down again and slipped out of the front door, shutting it quietly behind him.

The wind and rain came at him the moment he stepped out of the shelter of the porch. He walked slowly round the garden, bracing himself against the storm, revelling in the struggle with the elements. Clouds parted for a minute or two and there was a weird effect of moonlight in the wild night sky. Clive clung to one of the wrought-iron gates for support and stared at the outlines of hills and crazily lashing trees. He was wet through and he didn't care. The storm was beautiful. It was relentless but strong and true and healing.

I think I know now who's side I'm on, he said to himself. I don't think I'm going to swing round again. I feel mean about Jill, though. Perhaps I can help her some way even if I do go over to the enemy. Or perhaps she'll throw me over in any case as soon as she's got what she wants. I've not been much help to her tonight. Or perhaps I have. That pleased Reggie, her telling him about my letter to my father. How could I have written it? Why didn't I put it aside to think it over? It was the shock . . . you can't think straight when you've just had such a shock . . . If only I'd had Angela to talk it over with instead of Jill . . . It's upset Angy too. Poor Angy. It'll be nice having her as a sister. If she ever forgives me. Well, even if she doesn't I'm still on her side and on his. To have Reggie gloating over that rotten letter of mine . . .

The very memory made him shudder.

"If Reggie does any harm to my father I'll murder him," muttered Clive aloud, banging his hand against the gate. "I've got to stop him somehow. Well, at least I can warn them at the vicarage. Tonight? No, it's too late now, and Reggie isn't in a state to phone any of his journalist pals tonight. I'll go first thing in the morning."

He flung his head back to shake the wet hair out of his eyes, stepped on to the rung at the bottom of the heavy gate, kicked up the catch that was holding it open and let the wind swing it round with great force, carrying him with it. Then he did the same thing with the other gate, exulting like a child in the little rush of movement.

The two cars were still standing on the gravel. Felicity had forgotten, or been too busy, to put them into the garage. Clive peered into the Rover: the ignition key was in place. I'll put it away, he thought; it'll explain why I came out of the house and got wet.

Felicity and Jill were clearing away the dinner when he returned to the house.

"Where have you been?" they demanded in one voice.

"Putting the car away and shutting the gates."

"Oh." Felicity sounded a little mollified. "Thanks," she added ungraciously.

Clive carried trays and helped with the washing-up. When Felicity said she must go up to see how Reggie was, Jill clasped Clive round the waist and danced him about in a little jig.

"We're winning!" she cried. "She's got the wind up completely. And I'm in high favour, thanks to you. I'll work on Father tomorrow morning while he's getting over his hangover. I suspect he's getting a bit bored with her already and it won't take much to make him give her the final push."

"And what about the next one?" asked Clive. "The next one he marries?"

"Oh, I've got an idea about that too," said Jill mysteriously. "One thing at a time. You did your piece a treat, by the way," she added letting him go and standing back to regard him with exaggerated admiration. "You gave me a bit of a fright just near the beginning but after that—well, I couldn't have done better myself."

"Thank you," said Clive, making her a mock bow.

She smiled at him invitingly and for a moment he was afraid she was going to ask him to come to bed with her, which was the last thing in the world he wanted to do at the moment. But fortunately she gave a great yawn instead and said: "Well, it's all been rather exhausting, hasn't it? I'm for bye-byes. I bet there's not much of a love-nest in Father's room tonight. Wonder if Felicity won't be all that sorry to be out of it. Providing she gets some money, of course. I suppose she deserves a little. Anyway, we're going to talk about that in the morning. First operation crowned with modest success, Clive. Right?"

"Right," he replied firmly, feeling mean towards her and not knowing what to do about it.

11

At about a quarter past eight the following morning the rest of the household was sleeping soundly when Clive crept downstairs and made himself tea and toast in the kitchen. Then he let himself out of the back door and took big grateful gulps of the crisp morning air before walking at a quick pace in the direction of Southdene old village. The storm had cleared, leaving sky and sea and hills and all of nature looking freshly washed and shiningly new. They keep early hours at the vicarage, he said to himself; they are bound to be up and around by now.

His courage and determination held high while he waited an unconscionable time to cross the dual carriageway with its rush-hour traffic pouring into the Brighton urban area; but when he was over this obstacle at last and approaching the duckpond and the village green, he began to wonder what sort of welcome he was going to receive. Angela and her father would not be openly unkind, he felt sure, but there was a sort of dutiful charitableness which was almost worse than outright rejection or neglect. Clive had encountered a lot of this during his life, particularly from his uncle and aunt and from his mother's friends, and it had often made him flinch even more than Reggie's open hostility. If

Angela and her father were to treat him in this way it would be more than he could bear.

In the vicarage drive another small car was standing in front of the old green Mini. There can't be any visitors at this hour, surely, thought Clive as he came near to the front door. He put his ear close to it and heard the sound of voices. Resentment surged up, and fury that some other person could be receiving comfort and help and love from those who ought to be caring for him and him alone. He fought it back, reasoning with himself. He was not going to be much of an acquisition as a son and as a brother if the least little thing was going to drive him into a passion of jealousy. He must stick to his errand and get it over quickly and get back to the Old Manor before his absence could arouse suspicion, because he would be of more help to Angela and her father if he continued to keep a foot in both camps, at least for the time being.

Clive raised his hand and was about to press the bell when he suddenly remembered that he still had the spare key to the house in his anorak pocket. He took it out, and the little piece of metal gave him a sense of relief and reassurance out of all proportion to the significance of the fact itself. It was a symbol that he would be welcomed, that here was his home. He slipped the key into the lock and pushed at the heavy door.

"It's Clive here—may I come in?" he cried out, standing in the hall.

The sound of talking had come from the study: the vicar's voice called out through the half-open door in response to his cry. "Come on in, Clive. It's only our curate here. Come and meet him."

Clive relaxed in relief. There was not the least hint in Nevil's voice of that note of reluctant charity which Clive's over-sensitive ear was so quick to detect. And the visitor was only the curate, who would presumably be there as part of his job.

"I don't know whether you two have ever met each

other," said the vicar to the fair young man who had risen to his feet on Clive's entry. "Ronald Fenwick, Clive Bradley from the Old Manor who has been staying here for a little while until things are more settled for him."

"I've got a feeling we met once in the post office," said the Reverend Ronald Fenwick with the earnest determination of a shy man to overcome his shyness and perform his social duty. "That day there was a bomb scare and they turned us all out."

"That's right," agreed Clive. "I was trying to send off a parcel for my stepfather and it meant I had to take it all the way back again. I was furious, I remember. I'm afraid I swore about it a bit," he added, looking a trifle embarrassed.

"Oh well," said the fair young curate equally awkwardly, "it was very annoying. I was trying to send off an urgent registered letter myself."

"And it was all a hoax," said Angela, giving Clive a distinct wink as she left the room. "Shan't be a moment," she added. "I'm only replenishing the teapot. This place is like a cafeteria."

"I'll come with you," said Clive.

In the kitchen he said: "I'm sorry, Angy."

"Yes, you were rather bloody-minded, weren't you?" she replied, earning his eternal gratitude for not saying brightly and insincerely that it didn't matter, as so many other people would have done.

"I was foul. May I explain why?"

"If you like. Take a pew."

Angela poured out tea and seated herself opposite to Clive. They were in much the same positions as they had been on a previous occasion.

"Don't you want to go back to the study?" asked Clive.

"Lord no! Dad's only bringing Ronnie up to date with parish business and then they're both going off to have a session with the builder about the death-watch beetle in the church roof."

"Is it very bad?"

"The death-watch beetle? Frightful. We're in a permanent state of crisis."

"I wish I'd got some money to help."

"So do I. Never mind. We'll stagger through somehow or other. We usually do. Come on, Clive. Tell me all. I'm listening."

He told her all, tumbling it out in unfinished and disconnected sentences, the story of his life. When he came to the very recent past, however, he became more coherent, and Angela had a very fair idea of the situation up at the Old Manor and of Clive's motives for this early-morning visit by the time he had finished.

"How to silence Reggie," she said when he had done. "Have you any ideas, Clive?"

He shook his head. "Nothing unless I can get hold of the rest of that letter. I'm sure Mother wrote that Reggie was poisoning her."

"It sounds quite possible," Angela agreed.

"I don't think I'd better stay much longer now, Angy, much as I'd love to, because they'll all be awake and asking where I've been. I'll have to go on pretending to be angry with you and—" he gulped and took the plunge—"and with our Dad, because I'll learn nothing otherwise, but it'll only be pretence. You know that, Angy?"

"Of course. I don't know how you are managing to keep it up at all, this secret agent stuff. I'd never be able to do it. Good luck. Phone or pop down when you get the chance." They moved into the hall.

"And you'll tell him?" Clive jerked his head in the direction of the study.

"I'll tell him everything as soon as I possibly can."

"Thanks a lot. Sorry I've not had time to hear your life story," said Clive on the doorstep. "Next visit maybe?"

"You'll be sorry you asked!" Angela called after him laughingly as he ran down the drive.

I wonder, she said to herself, her smile fading as he

disappeared round the corner of the hedge; was it wise to let
him go back? What will he do?

Clive hurried back as quickly as he could, but it was still
much later than he thought when he glanced at his watch on
entering the grounds of the Old Manor. A new model
dark-coloured Rover was standing at the front door and
Clive glanced at it in some surprise: surely Reggie had not
been up and out already? He found Jill in the big drawing-
room, perched on the arm of a chair and turning over the
pages of a magazine in an irritated and impatient manner.

"Where the hell've you been?" she demanded.

"Getting some air. I woke with a stinking headache after
last night's show," replied Clive. To his surprise she
accepted this without question; she seemed to have something else on her mind.

"Car's out early," said Clive, jerking his head towards
one of the big windows.

"It's the doctor's," said Jill abruptly. "Father's sick."

"Good Lord."

"Not so very surprising, is it? Is it just ordinary sickness,
that's what I want to know."

"You don't mean that Felicity—" began Clive.

"Ssh. She's coming? Do your act. Chat her up. We're
very pally at the moment and I want to keep it that way until
I'm sure."

"Okay."

Felicity always made up her face with great care, but
there was no disguising the fact that she looked worried,
old, and tired to death. She made no comment on Clive's
arrival, but sank down into an armchair and said to Jill:
"What are we supposed to do now? Your father is con-
vinced that he is dying and he wants me to send for a priest
to hear his confession and perform the last rites."

"Oh for Chrissake!" groaned Jill. "Not all that circus
again! I wish he'd either stop having death-bed repentances
or stop getting divorced. It's a hell of a job to find a priest
who doesn't consider him excommunicated because of it.

D'you remember that time in London, Clive?—oh no, you weren't there—you'd been sent to that loony-school after having a go at Father with the breadknife. Your mother and I nearly went round the bend. In the end Pete and Tessa came to the rescue with a friend of theirs who was a black African minister working in race relations. He'd got so much worse problems to worry about that he didn't care whether Dad had sixty ex-wives. He was rather dishy, as a matter of fact," continued Jill with a reminiscent look coming into her eye. "I actually went to his church a couple of times. And he had the most extraordinary effect on Father. For at least three weeks after he got better he went about absolutely brimming over with Christian charity and forgiving everybody and writing huge cheques all round. Pity it didn't last longer," she concluded wistfully.

"Well, there aren't any dishy black African ministers in Southdene," said Felicity tartly, "so what are we going to do?"

"Send for the vicar, I suppose," said Jill.

That's no good. He hates him," said Felicity.

"Who hates who?"

"Hates whom," put in Clive, thinking that it would be noticed if he made no comment at all, and feeling that this was a safe thing to say. But underneath it he was simmering with fury against Jill. Fancy letting slip a reference to that ghastly time he had actually done Reginald physical injury! Or had she said it on purpose, to show Clive that she had a hold over him? Think of them at the vicarage, he told himself, and keep calm.

"Presumably they both hate each other," said Felicity. "I don't see how we could possibly ask Mr. Grey. I wonder if Father O'Connell would come along if I explained the situation?"

"No!" cried Clive and Jill in unison.

"But I don't suppose Reggie would mind," said Felicity defensively.

From time to time Felicity Westbrook found it convenient

to remember that she had been brought up a Roman Catholic. It had also occurred to her, more than once, that there would be certain advantages in converting Reggie to this faith. The indissolubility of marriage, for one thing. Reginald believing himself to be dying could be quite a promising candidate for conversion.

"No!" cried Clive and Jill again. "No Roman Catholics."

"All right then, I leave it to you," said Felicity, leaning back with an air of washing her hands of the whole matter.

There was a short silence.

"I know," said Clive breaking it. "Isn't there a curate?"

Felicity sat up and Jill looked at him in surprise.

"Would you believe it? The boy's actually had an idea."

"How do we get hold of him?" asked Felicity.

Clive shrugged. "Haven't the faintest," he replied.

"Perhaps the doctor will know. I'll ask him. He's still upstairs holding Reggie's hand."

Felicity left the room. Clive rounded on Jill.

"Why did you have to mention that time?" he demanded.

"Thought it would get you," replied Jill complacently.

"And I thought we were supposed to be working together."

"So we are. But there's no harm in cementing the union. I tell you what, Clive, I don't know whether or not Felicity is feeding the old man more drugs than he needs, and if so, whether the doctor knows it or not, but I've got a funny sort of feeling that something is about to happen, and if anything happens to Father and any questions are asked about it, then I don't want it forgotten that you and he have always been on the very worst of terms. That's all. See?"

"I can see that one can't trust you an inch in any direction," said Clive bitterly, "and I really thought you wanted to help me yesterday."

"That was yesterday, and I reckon you can trust me just about as much as I can trust you," retorted Jill, and for a moment they stared at each other in silence before turning to the door as Felicity came into the room.

"Dr. Jephcott's telephoning," she said. "He thinks he can do it more tactfully than me. It's rather a relief, I must say. He says he'll have to phone the vicar as a matter of etiquette, but that it will be quite in order to suggest that the curate should come along. In fact, considering what Mr. Grey must feel about Reggie, it seems only too likely that he'll make the suggestion himself."

It was with a great effort that Clive prevented himself from saying that it was fortunate that the curate was back from holiday.

"Is Reggie really very ill?" he asked Felicity, trying to recover his poise after the encounter with Jill, but feeling his whole body tingling with anger against her.

"He's had another heart attack," replied Felicity, "but Dr. Jephcott thinks the worst is over now and there's no reason why he shouldn't recover. Always provided he has complete peace and quiet and freedom from shock." She looked steadily at Jill and repeated: "Freedom from shock and strain. Family quarrels, that sort of thing, the doctor means. He's too weak to take it. And of course anything in the nature of the wrong sort of food or drink could be fatal at this moment. And the wrong sort of drug," she added thoughtfully.

"The wrong sort of drug," repeated Jill. "What would be the wrong sort?"

Felicity got to her feet. "Well, I'd better go and see what the doctor has fixed up," she said and left the room.

Jill and Clive looked at each other and their eyes signalled a temporary truce. "If that wasn't an invitation to attempt murder I don't know what is," said Jill. "She must be pretty sure of him. She's obviously got herself safely into that will of his. Or thinks she has. Wouldn't you think so, Clive?" she added, as Clive made no immediate response.

"What I think," he said at last very grimly, "is first, that she is the last person I'd want as a nurse if I was very sick. Second, that I am very anxious indeed to find out who fed the wrong drug to my mother; and, third, that I believe you know and I'm going to find out. I'm warning you, Jill Myrtle."

It was a fine dramatic flourish, but Clive spoilt it all by adding: "I wonder whether Reggie has left me anything in his will?"

—12—

The Reverend Ronald Fenwick was a good-hearted and sincere young man with a strong sense of vocation but without very much experience of dealing with his fellow-creatures. He longed to help and serve them, but was at heart still nervous of people and somewhat appalled by the odd quirks of human nature that were to be found even in an outwardly orderly and respectable parish like Southdene. Under the vicar's tactful guidance he was not doing badly, however, and Nevil had recently remarked to Angela that in a few years' time Ronnie was going to make a good parish priest, provided he could find the right sort of wife.

Angela had made a face.

"I am not suggesting," her father had added in his most sardonic manner, "that you in any way fit the bill. Although in fact," he added a moment later, "you could do a lot worse than Ronnie."

"Oh, he's all right," Angela had replied, feeling rather mean about having made that face, because she really did like Ronnie, "but he's too young to suit me. I'll look around for a nice meek and cosy little wife for him, shall I? Any ideas, Dad?"

"It's my job to marry people, not to find them marriage

partners," he had replied quite snappishly, and Angela had
said no more.

When the telephone call from Dr. Jephcott came through,
the two clergymen and the builder were standing round the
desk in the vicar's study, shaking their heads over the long
list of repairs that were needed for the roof of the church.

"Excuse me," said Nevil, lifting the receiver. "Who is it
speaking? Oh yes, Dr. Jephcott . . . you are at the Old
Manor now? Mr. Myrtle has been taken ill . . . yes I see.
You don't think he is really in any danger but it's a matter
of setting his mind at rest. Is that it? . . . Well, as a matter
of fact I am rather busy today, but Mr. Fenwick . . . He
happens to be with me at this moment."

Nevil put his hand over the mouthpiece and turned to the
curate. "Reginald Myrtle is very ill—or believes he is—and
he wants to make a confession and receive communion," he
said. "How do you feel about it, Ronnie? I must admit I'm
not particularly anxious to go myself. Mr. Myrtle and I met
yesterday and parted company in less than charity and the
doctor, terribly tactfully of course, thinks it might be a good
idea if someone else would undertake the office."

Ronnie looked distinctly scared for a moment before he
nodded and said: "Of course I'll go, Nevil. I'll have to
manage on my own one day, won't I?"

"I feel a bit of a pig, though, letting you go," said the
vicar after he had handed on the message and replaced the
receiver. "It's rather like throwing Christians to the lions.
Have you ever done any jobs up at the Old Manor, Bob?"
he asked, turning to the third man in the room.

The builder, a cheerful friendly person and a keen
member of Nevil's congregation, replied that he had, only
once, and that Mr. Myrtle had made an awful fuss about
paying the bill.

Nevil laughed. "That doesn't surprise me in the least.
From them that have shall not be taken away even what they
have. He appears to be feeling repentant, however, and no
doubt the vultures are hovering. Don't look like that,

Ronnie. That's human nature. You're going to see a lot of it. It doesn't mean they're beyond all spiritual help. We've got to believe they aren't and try and act on that. It isn't an easy option," he added as the curate still looked a little upset, "loving your fellow men in all circumstances. But you chose it, Ronnie. Excuse me a moment, Bob." He picked up a bunch of keys. "I'll have to go back to the church. We keep a little of the consecrated bread and wine there for such occasions."

Fifteen minutes later Ronnie Fenwick was backing his carefully-preserved Morris Minor out of the vicarage drive, and Nevil was saying to the builder: "It's cruelty to infants to send him into that den of thieves, but I couldn't see any other way."

"Well, Mr. Myrtle can't hurt him," said the builder comfortably, "not if he's as sick as all that."

"H'm," said Nevil. "I wish I could be so sure." Then he picked up the most expensive of the estimates. Come on," he said, "let's make a leap of faith and plump for total repair. No doubt the Lord will provide."

"You never know with the vicar," said the builder to his wife later that day, "whether he's taking the mickey out of you or being perfectly serious. If he weren't such a good man I reckon he could be a mighty bad one, if you see what I mean."

The apprehension that Ronnie Fenwick felt as he approached the Old Manor was not unmixed with more agreeable sensations. Like all people in a subordinate position, he sometimes had the feeling that he was being held back by his immediate superior. He had once suggested, when Nevil was particularly busy with other matters, that he should take on the job of visiting the sick Mrs. Myrtle for once, and the offer had been politely declined. Perhaps he was going to be allowed to do a bit more now, he thought hopefully. Not that he had any but the most friendly feelings towards the vicar, in spite of the fact that he did say outrageous things sometimes and you could never be quite sure that he was not laughing at you. And as for Angela—well, Ronnie could scarcely believe his luck when he first saw Angela. It was true that their private conversations had so far been mainly confined to the art of maintaining old cars, in which they were both keenly interested, but after all, that could be a beginning, and it was quite a usual thing for a vicar's daughter to marry her father's curate, from Charlotte Bronte downwards.

Ronnie was feeling quite cheerful as he drove through the open gates of the Old Manor. It would be something to tell John about when they next met. And John Martin, clerk to Messrs. Baslow and Snailes, solicitors of Brighton, would no doubt have something to tell him in return, because his firm was acting for the late Mrs. Myrtle.

Ronnie's first shock came when Jill answered the door. She looked him over appraisingly, decided that he was passable and would do for the occasional one-night stand if nothing better were to be had at the time, held out a hand and said: "I'm Jill Myrtle. It's my father upstairs who's writhing in agony and getting worried about his immortal soul."

"Do you want me to go straight up?" asked Ronnie.

"Sure. What else?"

Then Felicity appeared at the door of Reginald's bedroom. The fact that she was occupying it as well was only too obvious. Ronnie gritted his teeth; he was beginning to understand what Nevil had meant. He did not think he was particularly narrow-minded, and one had to take the world as one found it nowadays, but there was something about the sight and smell and feel of the overheated house and particularly messy-looking bedroom that gave him a faint sense of nausea. The most squalid of the slum dwellings that he had been to during his training had never given him this feeling: they had aroused pity but not revulsion.

However, there was a job to be done, and as Nevil had said, one had to believe that people were in need of spiritual help and do one's best.

Reginald ill was not a pretty sight. His yellow pyjamas did not go well with the pastiness of his skin or the purple rings round his eyes. The shifty, frightened look in the bloodshot eyes was not attractive either, and his mouth hung open loosely.

Dr. Jephcott, who had been standing by the bed holding Reginald's wrist, frowned as Ronnie came in.

"He's not fit to kneel down or anything, Mr. Fenwick," he said.

"There is no question of his kneeling," replied Ronnie, who knew the doctor slightly and felt somewhat reassured by his professional presence. "He need make no exertion."

"Well, so long as you understand that he is not to be placed under strain," said Dr. Jephcott somewhat ungraciously.

"I understand, sir," said Ronnie. And then he added, with a dignity that was all the more impressive for being quite unconscious: "I have watched people die."

"Um," said the doctor, rather taken aback, and Jill, Felicity, and Clive who had now all come crowding into the room, glanced at Ronnie with a mixture of unease and something approaching respect.

"If you would perhaps leave us alone now," murmured Ronnie, opening up the little casket he had brought with him and placing the delicate silver chalice on the dressing-table a few feet from the bed in which Reginald was lying.

With a little muttering and pushing the two women and Clive retreated through the door but remained hovering just outside it. Dr. Jephcott stayed at the foot of the bed, apparently reluctant to leave his patient.

"And you too, please, sir," said Ronnie firmly but politely.

"All right, but I'll be within call. Give me a shout if you notice the slightest change in his condition. I suppose you would notice," he added sceptically.

"It's part of our training," explained Ronnie patiently, "and I've done a St. John Ambulance course."

"Um," said the doctor again. "All right then. Be as quick as you can."

Ronnie poured some of the consecrated wine into the silver chalice.

A hoarse and agonized ` voice behind him whispered: "Please."

Ronnie turned to bend over the sick man. "What is it?"

"I want to pee—I've got to pee first," burbled Reginald.

"All right then."

Ronnie put an arm round the patient's shoulders and glanced around the room to see if there was a suitable receptacle. The group gathered outside the door had evidently heard the slight commotion because they all came hustling back into the room again. Ronnie explained the situation and Felicity took over. When Reginald had been made comfortable once more and the others had been got out of the room again, Ronnie, feeling distinctly agitated now, began the prayers.

"I've—I've done an awful lot of filthy things," muttered Reginald when invited to make his confession.

Ronnie listened patiently. His was a simple nature but there was nothing salacious in it. It gave him no satisfaction to hear the catalogue of Reginald's sins. Nevil's words were going through and through his mind: you simply have to believe that they need spiritual help and do your best. Well, he was doing his best, in very adverse circumstances.

". . . have mercy upon you, pardon and absolve you from all your sins," said Ronnie, at the same time as part of his mind was, in spite of itself, chewing over something that Reginald had just said.

"Hi, just a minute," muttered Reginald as Ronnie was proceeding to the next part of the service.

Ronnie bent his head to listen.

"In my pocket," whispered Reginald, feebly raising a hand to his chest. "Keep your back to the door—don't let any of them see."

There seemed to be no help for it. Ronnie extracted a few

crumpled sheets of paper from the pocket of his pyjama jacket.

"Managed to—hide it from them all," whispered Reginald with a faint note of triumph in his voice. "Want you to—keep it—in case I get better."

"Of course you will get better," said Ronnie, quickly concealing the paper in the folds of his cassock and laying a hand on the sick man's burning forehead. "Would you like to go on with the service now?"

Reginald managed a little nod: there was relief in his eyes.

Ronnie continued with the next prayer, but his thoughts kept returning to Reginald's words. Can it be true, can the man really be a murderer, Ronnie was asking himself as he raised the silver chalice to Reginald's lips. And at the same moment he thought: it's not for me to judge; I must try to forget it.

Reginald gulped at the consecrated wine like a greedy child and then collapsed against the pillows. Ronnie, with a hand on Reginald's brow, spoke the last prayer and then lifted the chalice to his own lips to drink the rest of the wine.

He was just about to drink when he heard a slight sound issuing from the bed. He placed the chalice on the bedside-table and put his fingers to the sick man's pulse. Then he lifted an eyelid and let it fall again, smoothing it down gently over the eye. His own face was very pale as he once more lifted the little silver chalice, this time to peer at and sniff at the remainder of the wine.

There was a scuffling at the door and four people burst into the room.

"Have you finished?" cried Clive and Jill.

"Is he all right?" cried Felicity.

"Stand aside, man, and let me see my patient," said the doctor.

"Will you please all keep back!" cried Ronnie, holding his arms out wide to prevent anyone coming any nearer. He was white and trembling but he stood his ground against the renewed onslaught. "Nothing is to be touched here—nobody is to come near. Will you all keep back and will somebody ring the police this instant. This instant!"

There was further uproar and at last Ronnie, becoming desperate, caught Clive's eye.

"All right," said Clive. "Hang on. I'll be back to help."

—*13*—

When Clive returned from telephoning, Dr. Jephcott was leaning over the bed, and Jill and Felicity were frantically attacking Ronnie, tugging at his arm to get at the silver chalice that he was holding out of their reach.

Clive rushed forward and caught hold of Jill.

"Are you mad?" he cried. "Do you want everyone to suspect you?"

"Suspect *me!*" screamed Jill. "*He* poisoned my father!" And she spat at Ronnie.

"He's just about the only person who didn't," said Clive grimly, giving Jill a shove towards the door before tackling Felicity, who bit his hand. Clive swore at her, sucked the sore place for a moment, and then looked at Ronnie, who had lowered the chalice slightly.

"Would you like me to take care of it?" said Clive. "I'll find somewhere safe from these hell-cats until the police arrive."

"Thanks," gasped Ronnie, "but I'd rather— if you don't mind—I think I'd better—hang on to it."

"Okay," said Clive. "I get the message. I'm a suspect too."

At that point the doctor looked up from the bedside.

"Nonsense," he said sharply. "There's no question of suspects. It's exactly as I anticipated. The whole business was too much for the patient. I knew it would be."

"You don't think he's been poisoned then?" asked Clive, and Jill, who had been standing whimpering near the door, raised her head.

"Of course not," said Dr. Jephcott firmly. "There's no question of it and there is no need to become hysterical." He turned to Ronnie and said with the air of a sensible man whose patience is very nearly at an end: "If you will kindly hand me that cup I can tell you in an instant whether or not there is anything wrong with the wine." And he held out his hand.

"I'm awfully sorry, Doctor," replied Ronnie, pale and trembling with shock but still standing his ground, "I'm sure you're right but I'd rather hang on to it if you don't mind."

"But this is preposterous!" exploded Dr. Jephcott. "I've never known such a thing in my life! Do you realize, young man, that I am a medical practitioner of many years' standing, that I am a member of the regional committee, that I act as adviser for—adviser for—" Words failed him. He was purple in the face and his mouth was opening and shutting like an outraged fish. "Are you presuming," he managed to say at last, "to question my qualifications or my reputation?"

"No, sir, not at all," replied Ronnie, more nervous than ever but still clinging to the silver cup.

"I should hope not indeed." The doctor drew out a handkerchief and mopped his brow. "Never known such behaviour," he muttered, "and from a clergyman too."

Clive suddenly laughed. "Bad luck, Doctor," he said. "In the battle of the professions round one goes to the Church. Triumph of soul over body, you might say."

"I don't know how you can talk like that," said Felicity, who had also found a handkerchief and was now crying in a ladylike manner, "with poor Reggie lying there dead."

"I can talk like that," said Clive, "because I'm not a bloody hypocrite like the rest of you. Saving your presence, of course, sir," and he made a little bow in the direction of Ronnie. "We're all of us delighted to see Reggie die. Whether any of us actually contrived it is another matter."

This produced another outburst from the doctor; Jill and Felicity also joined in, and all shouted at once.

Ronnie began to wonder how much longer he could hold out. If those women started scratching at him again, he would be sorely tempted to throw the rest of the wine in their faces and then knock them both out. He had been a keen boxer as a schoolboy and didn't think he had completely lost the art. But even more harrowing was the doctor's very justifiable fury. It was awful presumption on Ronnie's part not to let the older professional man take charge, and after all, with Reginald's soul departed from his body, the whole business was a medical matter now. While as for Clive, although he seemed to be on Ronnie's side, and the young curate really didn't know how he would have survived without him, nevertheless if one believed all the confession that Reginald had made, then Clive had the strongest motive of all for wishing him dead.

If only I can be proved wrong, thought Ronnie, I don't care how great a fool I look. And then in the midst of all his mental turmoil a new thought struck him that very nearly caused him to give in on the spot: why did it have to be somebody in this room who had, at great risk and not even having known that there would be an opportunity, slipped a drug into the wine? Why could it not be the man who had had all the time and opportunity in the world, who had access to the wine all along, who had actually given it to Ronnie? But it can't possibly be the vicar, he told himself: and the next instant he thought—why not?

He shut his eyes for a moment. The other four were still shouting at each other. Pray God I am mistaken, he prayed in as heartfelt a prayer as he had ever uttered in his life; let there be nothing wrong with the wine. He felt rather than

heard somebody coming towards him. He opened his eyes
again and there stood Felicity.

"Don't you think, Mr. Fenwick," she said, baring her
teeth in a far from sweet smile, "that you are rather
exceeding your duties?"

It's going to start again, thought Ronnie numbly, and
weakened by the suspicion that had just entered his mind,
he did not believe he could stand it much longer. He was
just beginning to wonder whether Clive had really tele-
phoned the police or had only pretended to do so and was
really part of a conspiracy to wear Ronnie down, when
blessed relief came in the sound of the front doorbell.

"I'll go," said Clive.

The tension in the room during his absence became
intolerable. Heat from the radiators, the heavy presence of
death, the smell of the passion and the fury of four
frightened people, all combined to create an atmosphere so
stifling that it was scarcely possible to breathe. Sergeant
Curtis, middle-aged, sceptical, not very pleased about this
call that had come when he was just about to go off duty,
walked into Reginald's bedroom and said: "Phew! Can't we
have some air in here?"

Clive pushed at the window.

"Now what's all this about?" said the sergeant in true
traditional style. His eye moved from Jill's scruffy clothes
to Felicity's barely-concealed hysteria, paused a moment at
the sight of Ronnie's cassock, and then came to rest with
relief on the only older man present.

Dr. Jephcott moved forward. "A little misunderstanding,
I think, Officer, on the part of our young reverend friend
here."

And he proceeded to give a fluent and extremely convincing account of the whole affair. Felicity and Jill visibly
relaxed, while Clive lounged against the end of the bed and
listened with a sneer on his face.

"Right," said the sergeant when Dr. Jephcott had finished. "Now, sir." He turned to Ronnie. "Let's hear your story."

Ronnie told it very nervously, conscious of hostile eyes, and the sergeant listened with ill-concealed scepticism.

"So you think somebody slipped some dope into the wine," he said at the end. "When would they have had the chance? You were left alone with the patient throughout the prayers, weren't you, sir?"

"Most of the time, yes, but there was one occasion—for several minutes," stammered Ronnie, "when I—I had my back to where I'd stood the cup ready filled—and when—I think—everybody came back into the room."

And he proceeded in the same intensely nervous manner to recount the little incident that the doctor had omitted in telling the story.

"You confirm this, sir?" Sergeant Curtis turned wearily back to Dr. Jephcott. "Mr. Myrtle asked to relieve himself and the prayers were interrupted for a short while?"

"Yes, that's right," said the doctor, frowning. "I'm sorry, Officer. I had forgotten for the moment. It was a very momentary interruption. Rather embarrassing really. Not the sort of thing one wants to remember on a solemn occasion like this."

"Probably not," said the sergeant, making a note. "Still, it happened. Now let me get this right." He turned back to Ronnie. "When the communicant has finished and before you give the final blessing you are supposed to drink the rest of the wine yourself if there is any left over. Is that right?"

Felicity gave a little gasp and Clive laughed. "It's a miracle there was any left after Reggie had been swigging it," he said.

The sergeant looked at Clive with displeasure. "I'm a Methodist myself," he said reprovingly, and then turned back to Ronnie.

"That's right," said the curate.

"It's essential that you should do this—those are your orders?" persisted the sergeant.

"Yes. That is what I am supposed to do." Ronnie, beginning to get a glimpse of the way the sergeant's mind was working, answered in a firmer voice.

"And it would take something very serious indeed to make you depart from routine?" went on the sergeant.

"Yes, very serious," said Ronnie.

"Such as really believing that if you drank the remainder of the wine you could poison yourself?"

"Yes," said Ronnie again, adding rather apologetically: "I know one isn't supposed to be thinking about such things at such a moment, but the instinct of self-preservation is very strong."

"Perhaps it's as well for you that it is," said the sergeant rather grimly. "On the other hand, it's odds on that there's nothing in it. Better just check, though. Won't take very long to get this analysed. If they're not too busy they'll do it today."

He held out his hand and with a feeling of great relief Ronnie yielded up the silver chalice and its dubious contents into the possession of the law. Well, it's out of my hands now, he said to himself, whatever comes of it. And whatever comes of it, surely Nevil will forgive me—surely he will know that I simply had to try to get at the truth.

A strange little sound issued from the other occupants of the room as the cup was handed over—something between a groan and a sigh. The doctor recovered himself first.

"If you wish me to do a post-mortem, Officer," he began, "I think I may have some free time tomorrow morning."

"Good of you to offer, sir," replied the sergeant. "We may well take you up on that." He glanced at the figure in the bed and appeared to ponder for a moment. "H'm. Bit awkward, this. Think I'll talk to my inspector. Can I use the phone?" He glanced at the telephone by the bedside.

"The extension's out of order," said Clive. "We have to go downstairs."

They left the room in single file, the sergeant coming last. He took the key from the inside of the lock, inserted it in the outside, and turned it and pocketed the key. "Sorry about this, sir," he said to the doctor who was standing nearest to him. "It's only for a little while. Just until I can have a word with my superior. He'll be glad to have a word with you too, if you don't mind."

The words were spoken. The upshot was that Reginald's body should remain where it was for the time being, but that the sergeant should have a look round the room on his own before opening it up again to the rest of the household. Dr. Jephcott's kind offer was noted with gratitude, and it was agreed that the death certificate should be held over until after the wine had been analysed.

It was while the sergeant was upstairs in the bedroom, and the doctor was on the telephone giving instructions to his receptionist, and the rest of them were standing around in the big drawing-room, uneasily avoiding each other's eyes and not speaking, that Ronnie was struck by yet another thought that almost caused him to exclaim aloud. He had told the sergeant nothing of the folded sheets of paper that Reginald had told him to take from the pyjama pocket and that were still safely concealed about the curate's own person. It was not just that he had not wanted to mention it in front of the others: he had genuinely forgotten.

But he wasn't really guilty of withholding vital evidence from the police, he thought when he became a little calmer, for surely this must be the letter that Reginald Myrtle had confessed to taking away before his stepson could read it. The letter that contained the startling revelation about the vicar that even now Ronnie was only just beginning to digest. And that very likely contained something else, something very damning about the sick man. "I took it," Reginald had gasped, "because I was afraid—it might say—something I didn't—want known." And then he had gone on to another subject before coming back to the letter and eventually muttering something about having hastened on his wife's death.

It had flashed through Ronnie's mind even while pro-
nouncing the absolution, what Nevil had once said: Extraordinary how even the sincerest penitent will slither about in
half-truths, still hoping somehow to get away with it. Shall
I read the letter, Ronnie asked himself, as soon as I get away
from here? Should it be considered as part of the confession? And in any case, just how privileged is a confession?
If there's been murder done—either by Reginald Myrtle or
of Reginald Myrtle—then won't it all have to come out?
Would John know the law on that? Or should he perhaps
give the letter straight to Clive, to whom it rightly be-
longed?

Ronnie was pondering all these problems when the police
sergeant returned to the room.

"That's all for now," he said. "If further enquiries prove
necessary, I'll get in touch with you all tomorrow. Sorry to
keep you so long from your patients, Doctor. And if I were
you, sir," he added turning to Ronnie, "I'd go and get
myself a stiff drink. You've had a nasty shock."

And with the very curtest of nods to Jill, Felicity and
Clive, the sergeant departed from the house.

Ronnie wasted no time in following him. The last thing in
the world he wanted now was conversation with any of the
others. Perhaps he would take the sergeant's advice before
going to see Nevil. The Black Swan, smallest and friend-
liest of Southdene's three inns, would still be open if he
made haste. And he was feeling hungry too, and could do
with a sandwich. The trouble was that the Black Swan was
a hotbed of village gossip, and Reginald Myrtle's death,
and the manner of it, was going to cause a tremendous buzz
of excitement. He would have to face people's curiosity
eventually, of course, but not just yet. Perhaps after all it
would be best to go straight to the vicarage. He was badly
in need of Nevil's advice, and Angela would produce some
refreshment and be sympathetic.

Ronnie got into his car, still a little undecided, turned
round on the gravel in front of the Old Manor, and drove

down the lane towards the dual carriageway. It was a steep and narrow lane, and entry on to the busy highway was always rather a hazardous operation, made no easier by the high hedge on the corner. Normally Ronnie was a good and careful driver, but the strain that he had recently undergone, coupled with his overall feeling of indecision, had perhaps weakened his concentration. He knew there was a car coming down the lane immediately behind him; a bigger and more powerful car than his own. He sensed that the driver was irritable and impatient and would be willing to take risks in getting out into the heavy traffic that he, Ronnie, would not want to take. And there was no room in the lane for the car behind to pass him.

The massive container lorries thundered by, with very little space between them. The driver in the car behind Ronnie hooted and hooted again.

Shut up, blast you, thought Ronnie: I can't possibly go yet.

And that was his last rational thought. He had the Morris in gear and his foot lightly on the brake, ready to shoot forward into the main road the moment the opportunity came. Something crashed into the back of the Morris with a spine-jerking force; brakes screeched, drivers screamed and cursed. The Old Manor side of the dual carriageway was packed with vehicles brought to a skidding, shuddering, nerve-shattering halt.

Ronnie saw nothing of all this. He was limply collapsed over the steering-wheel in the wreck of the little Morris, and the driver of the car behind, slightly bruised and shaken but nothing more, was bending over him with an expression of intense anxiety.

14

"It's a miracle you're alive," said Angela. And she laughed a little, with sheer relief, before adding very seriously: "But then I've always believed in miracles myself."

She stood up, leant over the hospital bed, and searched for a place among the bandages on the face to which to press her lips.

Ronnie, whose eyes had escaped without much damage, was dimly conscious of a heavenly vision in the midst of his hell of sickness and pain.

It seemed that his voice, as well as his eyes, was still just functioning. "My car," he croaked.

"It's in even worse shape than you are," said Angela. "Never mind. There are others to be had." She sat down by the side of the bed and smiled at him. "Don't try to talk," she said. "There'll be plenty of time for that later."

Ronnie's eyes closed, and Angela shut hers too for a moment. She was feeling a little dizzy, needing time to digest the series of shocks.

All those revelations yesterday, and then Clive suddenly turning up this morning wanting to be taken back into the fold. And then Reginald's illness, and the hasty phone call from Clive at the Old Manor that she had taken when her

124

father was out—a call saying no more than that Reggie had died and the police had been sent for, before the line had suddenly gone dead. Angela had not dared to ring back. Obviously somebody had come into the room and Clive had no further opportunity to talk without being overheard.

And then, later in the afternoon, had come the call from the hospital saying that Mr. Fenwick had been seriously injured. Angela had been surprised how much this news had shocked and distressed her. She'd scrawled a note for her father, leapt into the green Mini, and driven into Brighton in defiance both of the speed limits and of the capacity of the car itself. When she saw Ronnie she felt a great surge of compassion and tenderness. Whatever had been going on, at the Old Manor and elsewhere, one thing was absolutely certain: Ronnie Fenwick had harmed nobody; he was a completely innocent victim and he had simply got to get better.

A nurse came up to draw the curtains round the bed. Angela stood up. "Goodbye, dear Ronnie," she murmured. "They're going to operate on you now. I'll be here when you wake up. Goodbye for now. You're going to be all right. I promise you."

And she left the ward.

An elderly man in the bed opposite looked up from reading the evening paper and turned towards his neighbour.

"One of the crash victims," he said, indicating the curtained bed. "Right old pile-up this afternoon at the Southdene cross-roads. It's all here in the paper."

"Anyone killed?"

"Seems not." The elderly man began to read aloud. "'Three taken to hospital, one badly injured, two discharged after treatment. The driver of the lorry was unhurt and the driver of the Rover escaped with minor cuts and bruises.'"

"Shocking accident black-spot," said the occupant of the next bed indignantly. "Wonder how many more people will have to get smashed up before they put traffic lights. Anything else in the paper?"

"'Famous Author Dead,'" read out the elderly man. "Also at Southdene. Got itself into the news today all right, Southdene has. Reginald Myrtle—that's the fellow who writes those sexy spy stories. Hot stuff. Must've made a fortune." He read on a little and then exclaimed: "Well I'll be buggered!"

"What is it?" asked his neighbour, nearly falling out of bed in his curiosity.

"Would you credit it? Writes that stuff and yet he was very religious. Well I'll be—"

"What *is* it?" cried his neighbour again.

"Must've been a Roman Catholic or something near it," said the elderly man. "Died in the middle of receiving the last rites. Wonder if he'd had time to save his immortal soul. I bet it needed some saving."

"Here, gimme that paper!" cried the exasperated neighbour, tottering out of bed and grabbing it and then collapsing back against the pillows to read the story.

"Well I'll be buggered," he said also, after a moment or two. "Whole thing looks fishy to me. Wonder if someone bumped him off for his money."

The elderly man sniggered. "Maybe the priest poisoned the wine."

"Well, I wasn't exactly suggesting that," retorted the other. "Though mind you, they get up to some rum things, these people. Had a girl-friend once who was a Catholic. Scared stiff of Father Whatsisname, she was, howling fit to bust every time we'd been making a night of it. Dunno why she had to feel so guilty, because from what she told me about them—"

And he leaned over to whisper to his neighbour, who obligingly leant out of bed as far as he dared the better to appreciate the confidences.

"Well, Curtis," said the inspector after the sergeant had read the report from the analyst. "It looks as if we've got a case. The young curate was right. Not that that will be much comfort to him at the moment, poor devil. Any further news from the hospital?"

"Going on as well as can be expected," was the reply. "He'll be on the danger list for some time, though, and it doesn't look as if we'll be able to talk to him very much for a while."

"We may have to face it," said the inspector, "that we're not going to get very much information from him at all. Depends how bad the concussion is. Rotten luck to go and smash himself up like that immediately after the business at the Old Manor. Shock of it all had made him a bit careless perhaps. Or just a bad driver."

"He'd had a shock all right," said the sergeant slowly, "but he didn't strike me as the sort to be careless about other people's lives. You should have seen him standing up to those women, and the doctor and all. Easiest thing in the world just to say he'd been mistaken and let them throw away the rest of the wine. Everyone would have been delighted. Doctor would have signed the certificate. No trouble at all, and another undetected murder. But no. He's got a conscience and some courage, that youngster. Credit to his profession."

"Well, well." The inspector was amused. It was rare for Sergeant Curtis to bestow such praise. "Do I detect in you the first symptoms of a conversion?"

"I'm a Methodist myself, sir, as you know," said the sergeant, reverting to his usual stolid manner. "I thought when I first got there that the young man was just being hysterical, like some of those over-eager young Anglo-Catholics sometimes are. The doctor's story seemed plain enough. But when I saw the way the others were behaving, and when I'd talked to Mr. Fenwick a little myself, well, I began to revise my opinion, as I told you, sir. And there's another thing."

"Go ahead," said the inspector.

"Somebody had dissolved those sedative tablets in the

wine. Not enough to kill a healthy person, but enough to kill a sick man, particularly one with a serious heart condition. Let's take it that the curate was not intended to die too. Then either our poisoner didn't know that the priest had to drink the rest of the wine, or else he knew that, but knew it wouldn't kill him."

"So he—or she—either possesses both ecclesiastical and medical knowledge or is ignorant in both fields," commented the inspector. "It's a line to work on."

"But everyone knew," continued the sergeant, "that the sick man wanted to confess his sins and by all accounts he had plenty of them. Now, confessionals are privileged communications, of course, but there may be circumstances in which such privilege doesn't hold—or at any rate the person concerned may have feared so."

"Ah, now we're coming to it," said the inspector. "You think our young priest may have carried away from the house a dangerous secret in his bosom? Perhaps without even knowing that he possessed it?"

"Perhaps without even knowing that he possessed it," repeated the sergeant. "But somebody might have suspected that he did, and somebody might have been very afraid it could go further."

"And drove down the lane after him and bashed into the back of his car at a vital moment, shoving him a couple of yards forward into a lorry. Taking a frightful risk, wasn't it? Could have broken his—or her—own neck, not to mention several other people's."

"People do take risks when they're desperate," said the sergeant.

"Very true. We'd better have another look at the reports on that accident, then."

"I'm very sorry to have to bother you about this business, sir," said Sergeant Curtis the following morning to the vicar of St. Mark's Church, Southdene. "It must be most distressing for you."

"It is indeed," replied Nevil. "I shall never forgive myself for sending Ronnie Fenwick out on that job."

"He seems to be making good progress, I'm glad to say," said the sergeant, "though actually that was not quite what I meant." He paused a moment, not certain of the most tactful way to proceed.

"Please don't trouble to be delicate." Nevil produced cigarettes and motioned the sergeant to a chair. "I assure you that as far as I am concerned, you can ask what you like and it won't worry me at all. The whole village now knows that Clive Bradley is my son and that I quarrelled with Reginald Myrtle about it and that he threatened me with exposure. I imagine most of them have also made the obvious connection by now, and by mid-day there will be no doubt at all that I murdered Mr. Myrtle. They are having the time of their lives. I never expected to provide so much of a thrill for so many people at once."

"I see, sir," said the sergeant noncommittally. Was this airy manner only superficial, he wondered: was there bitterness and even pain beneath, and perhaps also some apprehension? It was difficult to imagine the vicar ever being afraid of anything, but then, as the sergeant kept reminding himself, Mr. Grey was a very good actor.

"If you could just show me for a start, sir," he asked, "where the communion wine is kept and what you do when you have an urgent call such as the one from the Old Manor."

"Right. We have to go over to the church. Be prepared for some of the limelight."

There were, indeed, considerably more people than was usual on a Saturday morning hanging around by the lych-gate, peering at inscriptions on ancient tombstones, and inspecting the east window and the splendid roof and the other beauties of the church. Many of them greeted the vicar and he responded with cheerful politeness, but after the two men had passed by, several eager little conversations broke out.

"It is a matter for speculation in the village," remarked Nevil calmly to the sergeant as he unlocked the vestry, "whether or not Clive resembles me in appearance. I shall be interested to hear the final verdict and so, no doubt, will he."

He's certainly a cool customer, thought the sergeant as he noted the arrangements for reserving some of the consecrated wine. As they talked he found himself coming to much the same conclusion about Nevil as the builder had arrived at: he's a very good man by all accounts but I wouldn't like to cross him—something very tough and ruthless hidden there.

"I see, sir," he said aloud. "And there's no locks been tampered with, or keys missing?"

"Nothing at all."

When they were back in the study at the vicarage, the sergeant said: "I shall have to ask you, sir, about this interview you had with the deceased."

Nevil readily described the brief talk with Reginald.

"And your daughter, sir? Did she know about Mr. Myrtle's threats?"

For the first time there appeared just the faintest trace of a crack in the vicar's composure.

"Yes," he said after a slight hesitation. "My daughter was fully aware of the position. You will want to talk to her. She's at the hospital at the moment, visiting Mr. Fenwick, but she will be here this afternoon."

"Then there's just one more thing I have to ask, purely as a matter of form, you understand. Do you have any bottles of any sort of tranquillizers or similar such drugs in the house?"

"We're not great pill-swallowers here," replied Nevil. "My daughter enjoys the rudest of health and I'm not often ill apart from the occasional bout of bronchitis. We've got—let me think—aspirin of course, but presumably that doesn't count. A linctus with some morphine in it that I've been taking at nights to ease a cough, and a few lozenges and vitamin tablets. I should think that's about all. Oh no, of course. I forgot. Dr. Jephcott wrote out a prescription for Clive to calm him down when he was in a state of great agitation after his mother's funeral. It's no use asking me what it was for," he went on, anticipating the sergeant's next question, "because I didn't notice. Neither did Angela. And it wouldn't have meant anything to us even if we had been able to read the doctor's writing. The only thing I do remember is that he said it was a new drug and it should not be used for heart cases but that didn't apply to Clive. I dropped the prescription in at the chemist myself and Angela collected it. There were about fifteen or twenty white tablets, as I remember."

"And did Mr. Bradley take any of them?"

"One or two. My daughter will remember exactly. They certainly seemed to be very speedy and effective."

"And would you by any chance know, sir," asked the sergeant casually as he made a little pretence of glancing back through his notes, "what became of the balance of the tablets?"

"It so happens that I do," replied Nevil with equal unconcern. "After Clive had apparently decided that he wanted no more to do with us, I came across the bottle on the kitchen window-sill and I flushed the lot down the lavatory. Am I not right in thinking that is what the pharmacists would like us all to do?"

"Yes, indeed, very wise precaution," said Sergeant Curtis, ignoring the distinct note of mockery in the vicar's voice. "Pity more people don't throw away their unwanted medicines."

But that's not the story that the young man told me, he was saying to himself. Clive Bradley said he took the bottle with him to the Old Manor and destroyed the rest of the tablets there. Now which, if either, is speaking the truth? Which one of them is trying to protect the other?

"That'll be all for the moment, then," he said. "I'll call in later to see Miss Grey."

Angela turned up only a few minutes after the sergeant had departed. "Ronnie's perked up no end," she reported. "He's getting quite chatty. Doesn't remember much about the crash or what led up to it, but he keeps muttering something about a letter he thinks he ought to have. It seems to be worrying him. But we never told him about *the* letter, did we, Dad?"

"No, but I suppose he might have heard something from one of them at the Old Manor."

"We'll ask Clive. He's coming to lunch, by the way. I met him outside Martha's Pantry just now holding court to three old ladies at once. He seems to be basking in the sunshine of unaccustomed popularity. Or curiosity," she added after a moment's thought.

"He'll have to get a job," said Nevil.

Angela laughed. "Poor Clive. He'll be longing for the good old easy-going days of Reginald."

The lunch was a surprisingly cheerful meal for three people under a cloud. Nevil and Angela related some parish scandals and Clive reported on the state of affairs at the Old Manor.

"It will be better when we know the provisions of Reggie's will next week," he said. "This now forms the main topic of conversation—if such a succession of little poisoned darts can be called conversation—between Jill and Felicity. Speculation as to the identity of the poisoner has died down since the police were there this morning. But of course we are all suspecting each other like mad and no one will eat anything that has been prepared by anybody else. This makes for frightful traffic jams in the kitchen at meal times. It's a treat to sit down to a civilized lunch."

Angela wanted to know how Jill was bearing up.

"So-so. Lethargy interspersed by flashes of hysteria," said Clive. "I'm sorry for her," he went on, "although she's a nasty little bitch. She's terribly lonely. Pete and Tessa are coming down this afternoon. That'll help a little. Oh, and I've had the most extraordinary talk on the telephone with

Aunt Sarah in Yorkshire. It went on for hours. I got her to reverse the charges so that Reggie's estate will have to pay for it. Might as well get that much out of him, if nothing else. She kept promising to Stand By Me in capital letters. She obviously thinks I murdered Reggie. So does the sergeant. Very interested in those knock-out pills that the doc prescribed for me. Oh, sorry. Aren't we supposed to talk about it?"

He looked from one to the other. Angela and Nevil, who had been listening with mild amusement to what he was saying, had suddenly become very still and there was strain in the room.

"Sorry," said Clive again, getting up and assembling crockery. "I'll wash up. What happens in a vicarage on Saturday afternoon?"

"Dad does his accounts and writes a sermon and I either go out or do some gardening," said Angela. "And the phone and doorbell rings rather a lot."

"I could help with the gardening, perhaps," said Clive.

"You can start clearing that patch by the side-gate," said Nevil getting up from the table. "We need some more space for vegetables. Or rather," he added with great emphasis, "my successor will no doubt be glad of it, and I should like to hand over the premises in tolerable order."

"What was that last bit about?" asked Clive when the vicar had left the room.

"I don't know. He's never mentioned it before," said Angela.

"But he can't just give up like that!" burst out Clive in one of his sudden flashes of uncontrollable fury. "He loves his job and he's super at it. I thought the Church was supposed to be broad-minded nowadays. Even if they don't like mud-raking, surely they could make an exception?"

"I suppose it all depends," said Angela slowly, "on what it is that they have to make an exception about."

"So you agree about the cause of death, Doctor?"

Sergeant Curtis looked round the tastefully-furnished

sitting-room of the elegant modern Georgian house over-looking the village green. Mrs. Jephcott, too, looked as if she had stepped out of the pages of an ideal home magazine, and a teenage girl dressed in very smart riding gear had just walked past the window.

"In essentials, yes," said Dr. Jephcott. "There are one or two points of detail—but, however. Yes. In essentials I agree." His manner was confident enough but his hands were very restless, the sergeant noted. "I'm afraid I misled you at first, Officer," he went on. "To tell the truth, I didn't believe the young curate. I thought he was being a little hysterical. The priesthood does tend to attract some rather unbalanced types at times, you know."

"Yes, sir," said the sergeant. "That was my opinion too, at the start of it."

"But of course we have now been proved wrong." The doctor stabbed out yet another half-smoked cigarette. "I wish I could help you further, but I really can't see how. Needless to say, I myself certainly saw nobody tamper with the wine."

"No, sir, I am sure you didn't," said the sergeant.

"And it's hardly to be supposed that the young curate did so himself—how is he, by the way? I meant to call in at the hospital but haven't had a moment."

"Going on nicely, sir," was the reply. "Thanks partly no doubt to your expert and speedy first-aid work after the accident."

"All in a day's work," said the doctor.

"I suppose you didn't by any chance, sir, when you were examining him in the car, notice anything drop from his clothing? Some folded sheets of paper—anything like that?"

Dr. Jephcott frowned. "Drop from his clothing? I am afraid I don't understand you, Sergeant. The boy was unconscious and obviously badly injured. He was all twisted up with the steering-wheel. The car was a wreck. I can't imagine that any of the rescue workers could have been bothering about bits of paper at such a moment. I most certainly was not."

"No, of course not, sir. Sorry to trouble you." The sergeant got up to go. "You aren't by any chance a churchgoer, sir, are you?" he asked casually.

"Afraid not. Had too much of it as a boy. Carol service at Christmas, of course," was the reply.

"I hear your vicar here preaches a very good sermon," said the sergeant. "Perhaps you ought to go and listen to him some time."

And he took his leave.

15

Evensong at St. Mark's, Southdene, was usually well attended. People could be sure of having some of their favourite hymns, and ones that were not too difficult to sing, and Nevil never preached for long and often said things that made you want to laugh and he didn't seem to mind if you did laugh. It tended to be a cheerful occasion that left people feeling a little less gloomy about the state of the world and a little more willing to tolerate people they were annoyed with—for a few hours, at any rate.

On the Sunday after Reginald Myrtle's death the church was exceptionally full, and regular attenders noticed many unfamiliar faces. In one of the pews near the door sat a young reporter from a national daily paper; he was hoping for a nice little human interest story to follow up the bit he had done on Reginald Myrtle's death, and he had dragged along his grumbling girl-friend who had had other ideas for seeking amusement that evening. During the opening prayers she did a great deal of ostentatious yawning, but when the slightly trembling, bell-like voices of the younger choir-boys rose in the Magnificat she stopped fidgeting and slumped back in the corner of the pew, staring at the east window and listening with a dreamy and somewhat foolish expression on her face. Her boy-friend gave her an amused glance and she hurriedly shifted and yawned again.

The hush of expectancy when Nevil stepped up into the pulpit would not have disappointed a leading actor on a famous stage. Surely, they thought, he would not let them down: something must be said.

"My text for this evening," said Nevil in his most deceptively benevolent manner, "comes from the seventh verse of the eighth chapter of the gospel according to St. John: 'He that is without sin among you, let him first cast a stone . . .'"

Ah, thought the young reporter, surreptitiously scribbling on a little memo pad that he had propped up against a hymnbook: that's one in the eye for the local scandal-mongers—I'm going to enjoy this. But after a little while his expression of detached amusement faded and he put away his pencil with a furtive gesture; while his girl-friend was staring at the preacher as if hypnotized, her mouth slightly open and in her eyes a noticeable expression of alarm.

Fifteen minutes later the whole congregation, uneasily searching their consciences and remembering far too many things that they wished they had not said or done, reached for their hymnbooks and shuffled to their feet. The organist played a phrase, and the congregation burst into the first verse of "Abide with Me" in as fervent a plea for comfort and mercy as the ancient church had ever heard.

"Bernie," whispered the reporter's girl-friend, tugging at his arm. "I wish I'd never written that letter to Mum."

"You ought to go to church more often," he whispered back unsympathetically. "It might make you think a bit more." But he was still looking a bit uncomfortable himself.

Nevil came round to the church porch and shook hands with many of the departing congregation. The strangers saw only a kindly middle-aged clergyman who seemed genuinely grateful to them for coming to his church. It was as if the powerful, moving, and sometimes frightening exhortation to judge not that they be not judged, had never been. But most of them went on their ways very thoughtful. At least for the time being.

"Well, that was a star performance all right," said Clive, laying out cutlery on the table in the vicarage kitchen. "Did you see poor Jilly? She sneaked out after the sermon. I never saw her look so conscience-stricken. A real tour de force," he continued chattily. "Pity they don't have curtain calls in churches."

"It was a piece of sheer devilment," said Angela, angrily hacking at the cold joint and looking up to glare at her father. "Meant to work on people's feelings and get someone to confess. Was it your own idea or did you cook it up together with the police? Did you? Did you?" she insisted.

"I myself have been the subject of some rather malicious gossip," said Nevil, placidly accepting a plate. "It is a well-known axiom of warfare that the best method of defence is to attack."

"Oh, you're impossible!" Angela flung down the knife and fork and ran out of the room.

"What's the matter with her, Dad?" asked Clive. "I thought Angy was immune to these sort of female tantrums."

Nevil made no reply.

"It's not been the same, has it," said Clive, looking shrewdly at his father, "since Angy learnt about me."

"No, it hasn't been the same," agreed Nevil. And then he added, very seriously: "Perhaps it's just as well."

Clive looked as if he were about to continue with the subject, but then suddenly changed his mind.

"As a matter of fact I have got something I ought to tell you," he said. "It's about those tablets the doctor gave me when I was rampaging about the place—for which I'm very sorry, by the way, I must have been an awful nuisance and I'll try not to be one any more. I know we've all been very carefully not mentioning them, since it appears that they were similar, if not the very same, as the ones that killed Reggie, but I would like to tell you now if I may."

"Tell me by all means," said Nevil, "though I think I can guess."

"Well, the police asked me about them of course, and I said I'd taken them to the Old Manor with me and thrown them away there. But actually I never saw them at all. Angy gave me one out of the bottle, and that's all I know about the tablets."

Nevil smiled faintly. "And that's all I know either," he said, "although I told the police exactly the same story as you did."

"Then you don't possibly think that Angy—?"

"She hasn't mentioned it to me, but I think it very likely that she told the police that she was the one who destroyed the rest of the tablets."

"Then if she said so, it means she did. Angy wouldn't tell a lie," said Clive. And then, a moment later: "Or would she?"

"I think," said Nevil, "that the best thing you and I can do is to try very hard to believe that Angela destroyed the rest of those tablets. It is surprising what you can believe when you really put your mind to it. Incidentally, she is quite right in thinking that I am hoping there will be some reaction to that somewhat melodramatic sermon of mine. I didn't actually cook it up with the sergeant, as she suggested, but the sergeant and I understood each other very well when we had our second chat yesterday afternoon."

The hope was not in vain. It was about six o'clock the following evening when Jill rang the front doorbell of the vicarage. Clive and Angela had gone to the hospital to visit Ronnie and Nevil was alone.

"I don't know whether I'm disturbing you," said Jill, awkwardly shaking hands and then looking round with unseeing eyes at the old red curtains, the shabby armchairs, and the blazing logs. "I nearly funked it again at the last moment but Pete and Tessa said I'd got to come. They drove me down on their way to Brighton and they're collecting me again in about an hour but I'll get out of your way before then and go and wait somewhere else. It's an awful nuisance not having a car, but of course now I've got all that money I can buy what I like."

She was talking quickly and jerkily, constantly glancing at the door as if she would love to run out of the room. Nevil offered her a cigarette.

"Thanks. I don't mean I've told Pete and Tessa what it's about," she went on in the same intensely nervous manner. "I just told them there's something I ought to've told somebody ages ago and I felt I couldn't bear it any longer unless I told somebody now, and they said did I want to tell the police but I didn't fancy it much because it's probably perjury or something and I've got a bit of a thing about the possibility of going to prison, I mean I can't stand being shut up anywhere and having people tell me what to do. I can't stand it!"

Her voice rose in a threat of hysteria.

"Neither can I," said Nevil soothingly. "Would you like a drink of any sort?"

Jill shook her head. "Haven't really fancied anything since—since—" Her voice faded away and then it all came out in a rush. "It was one hell of a shock," she cried, "seeing my father die like that! I mean they all think I hated him and only wanted his money and I did in a way and I didn't see why anyone else should have it after all my mother was his first choice and it wasn't her fault she didn't have a son and if he'd only been a bit more patient and waited a bit she might have and in any case there was no need to be such a bastard to her and he might at least have seen she was decently provided for because he was as mean as hell you know except when he got sick and started worrying about eternal damnation but all the same I'd got no one else of my own and it's a funny sort of thing this family business—"

She ran out of breath and threw her barely-touched cigarette into the fire before going on.

"Anyway you'll understand all about that with this business of Clive because he's had a rotten time too really and I've not exactly helped him but I would like to help him a bit if I can now I've got all this money and I'm awfully glad he's found you only I can't help envying him because there's no one left for me to find, but I must shut up because that's not what I came about and if there's one thing I absolutely cannot stand it's self-pity."

Jill shook her head violently and rubbed a hand across her eyes. Nevil lit a cigarette and waited.

"At least Father kept his promise and left me the cash," she went on after a moment. "You've got to hand him that. And in a way he was sorry, I think. I mean, he'd got the most awful hang-ups about his own childhood—I can hardly remember my granddad but he was a real hell-fire priest, I believe. It's no wonder my father reacted against it. But he shouldn't have got the doctor to give all that extra dope to Clive's mum. That was a beastly thing to do and I wish now I'd told somebody about it before instead of keeping it to myself. But I always do think first of myself, I'm afraid, and of course when I read it through I thought, ah, here's a hold over Father and over the doctor too. I'll just keep quiet about it for the time being and see what use I can make of it. You never know when things will come in useful."

Jill was talking more calmly and steadily now and Nevil thought it was probably safe to do a little gentle prompting.

"You did read the whole of the letter that Clive's mother wrote to him, then?"

"Well, of course I did. Who wouldn't? And I copied it all too." Jill dug into the pocket of her dirty lamb's-wool jacket and produced a crumpled piece of paper. "This is the last sheet. I pretended to Clive that I knew nothing about it. It was partly that I wanted to use it for myself and partly that I didn't want him to be upset and partly that I didn't trust him. I mean, he can be pretty violent at times, Clive, and I was scared that he'd really murder Father and probably the doctor too if he knew. Which maybe he did. Kill Father, I mean," said Jill shaking her head again. "I mean, he'd got enough against him even without his mother's letter. And so had the doctor—Father used to treat him like dirt—and so had several other people," she added awkwardly.

"Including myself," said Nevil. "May I read it, please?"

Jill held out the crumpled paper.

"Yes," said Nevil presently. "Yes, that looks plain enough. Maureen clearly had no doubt that her husband and the doctor were in league together to procure an earlier death than might otherwise have occurred. It ties in with certain hints that she dropped during those last weeks that I was visiting her. If it's any comfort to you, she really wanted to die. Morally and legally of course, that doesn't make any difference."

"I don't reckon there was much mercy killing about it," said Jill. "Father just wanted to be finished with her. He had no patience at all. Just like me. And he loved playing on people's weak points. Just like me again."

"I wonder," said Nevil following up his own train of thought, "which of them was actually responsible for Maureen's death."

"I should think Father got the doctor to agree to give her an overdose," said Jill. "He wouldn't do anything himself. He never liked dirtying his hands if he could get somebody else to do it for him."

"It must have been a very heavy piece of persuasion," said Nevil. "Presumably he must have had some hold over the doctor. Have you any idea what it could be?"

"Abortion racket perhaps," replied Jill. "Or the doctor's lady-friends. That'd put paid to his nice family man image. Or maybe he'd made some sort of a balls-up over a patient in his youth. I expect there's a dossier on him tucked away among Father's papers somewhere. I'll have a look if you think I ought to."

"I'm afraid I do think you ought to," said Nevil, "distasteful though the whole business is. It may prove to be important evidence. And this copy of Maureen's letter may be important too. Would you swear in court that it is a true copy?"

"Oh, my God!" Jill looked very alarmed. "Would I have to? I'm scared stiff of going to court. I'm scared stiff of a lot of things as a matter of fact. Of dying, for one."

"I'm sorry," murmured Nevil.

Jill looked up at him suspiciously. "I'd like to tell you if you'll promise not to laugh at me. Clive says you're awful for laughing at people."

"My dear child," said Nevil, distressed. "I most certainly promise not to laugh."

Jill talked for several minutes. Eventually she said: "I'm getting as bad as Father. A tendency to confessing seems to run in the family. But I'm not just trying to attract attention," she suddenly blazed out, "and I do need help!"

"You are not just trying to attract attention," repeated Nevil very seriously, "and you certainly need help."

There was a short silence.

"I suppose you're going to tell me to take this to the police," said Jill.

"The police will certainly have to know about it," replied Nevil, "and I don't think you will find yourself much blamed for not having come forward with it sooner. I am wondering, though, whether there isn't some way of letting them know without bringing you in."

Jill looked up hopefully.

"I think it rather depends," continued the vicar, "on what Ronnie Fenwick is able to tell us. Will you leave this with me?"

Jill indicated that she was only too delighted to be rid of the crumpled sheet of paper.

"I'm going to see Ronnie tomorrow morning," said Nevil. "Don't say anything about this if the police ask you again, but give me a ring about lunch-time. All right?"

Jill, unused to expressing gratitude, managed to say that it was very much all right and got to her feet.

"Pete will be here in a minute and I'd better go," she said, but it was obvious that there was still something troubling her. "If he's talkable to—Ronnie Fenwick, I mean," she said at last, "d'you think you can tell him I'm sorry about the way I behaved to him after Father died? It was all such a shock. Of course I couldn't help wondering whether Father had mentioned anything when he was making his confession, and where the original of the letter was, and then I thought the doctor must have killed Father for fear he might talk about the other thing, and then I thought, no, it's more likely Felicity because she knows all about drugs too; and then I wondered about Clive, and then I wondered about you, and then I wondered about the doctor again and I suddenly thought, My God, suppose the doctor finds out what I know about him, he's going to kill me too—and I was absolutely terrified and it seemed to me much the best thing would be if Father had just died naturally."

"Yes, I see," said Nevil. "Are you less terrified now?"

"Um. Yes, I think I am," said Jill with an air of surprise.

Nevil arrived at the same time as Sergeant Curtis outside the side ward to which Ronnie had been removed.

"After you, sir," they said at the same moment and then both laughed.

"I'd rather you talked to him first, honestly," said the sergeant. "I'll go down to Out-Patients and get a cup of coffee."

"You're not afraid I'm going to persuade him to suppress vital evidence that could be used against me?" said Nevil.

"Sir!" The sergeant's outraged exclamation was in the nature of a reproof and Nevil looked a little shamefaced.

"I'm sorry," he said. "I'm afraid it brings out all the worst in one's character, being suspected of murder."

Ronnie still looked a wreck, but a surprisingly cheerful

and contented wreck. He was delighted to see Nevil and quite fit to talk, but the difficulty was to turn his conversation to any other topic than Angela.

"She's promised to come to the car auction," he said, "when I'm fit again. We're rather taken with the idea of an old Renault, though I doubt if we'd get one there. But she thinks it would be rather fun."

This seemed to promise a way into the subject that Nevil wanted to talk about. "Ronnie," he said firmly, "what is the last thing you can remember before the crash?"

"Blue Rover," said Ronnie promptly, "coming along behind. Don't suppose we'll ever be in a position to have a Rover." he added wistfully.

Nevil controlled his impatience with the man who looked more and more like being his future son-in-law.

"And before that," he said. "What were you planning to do with that letter?"

"Letter? What letter?" Ronnie looked dazed. Doctors and nurses had warned that his memory was still very patchy and uncertain.

Nevil produced some folded sheets of paper: the one at the bottom was very crumpled.

"Now listen, Ronnie, listen very carefully," he said. "I am going to read you a true copy of the letter that Reginald Myrtle confessed to stealing from his stepson before Clive had read it. I am going to read the whole of it very slowly, and then I want to ask you some questions."

"Yes," said Ronnie, and then instantly added: "Is Angela coming this morning?"

"She's coming in about an hour's time," said Nevil, feeling exceedingly uncharitable towards the lovesick and injured young curate, "and she won't be pleased if you've not helped about this letter."

After a few more references to Angela, Ronnie was induced to co-operate, and a tolerably full account of Reginald Myrtle's last words on earth was at last conveyed from the curate to the vicar. Unfortunately Ronnie, his mind now firmly diverted away from Angela and old cars, began to worry about the lost letter again and he even tried to get out of bed as if he proposed to go and look for it at this very moment.

"It must be somewhere on the floor of the car," he cried. "Can't they look for it there?"

Nevil had as hard work to soothe him as earlier he had had to rouse him, but at least he was now in possession of some useful information and in due course Sergeant Curtis was suitably grateful. He was also grateful for Jill's suggestion that her father might have kept a dossier on Dr. Jephcott, but in spite of all her efforts to find it, nothing came to light.

"I suppose the doctor must have found the papers himself while my father was ill," said Jill at last. But she wasn't really satisfied with this explanation and she continued to brood about it after the sergeant had departed to report back to his chief.

"What I think must have happened," he said to the inspector, "is that the doctor panicked when he heard that Mr. Myrtle wanted to make a confession, and he took an unexpected opportunity of doping the wine—not realizing, perhaps, that the priest was supposed to drink any left over. It was quite clever, and not really all that much of a risk, because nobody would have been surprised if the patient had suffered a fatal heart attack and nobody would have queried the death certificate."

"But even if he'd got away with that," protested the inspector, "that still left the priest with the dangerous secret, as we said before."

"Yes, sir, and as we said before, the killer then panicked even more, and crashed his car into the back of the curate's, which meant that he was first on the spot to give first-aid and to find and remove the letter which Mr. Myrtle had given to Mr. Fenwick. Yes, I know it sounds crazy and far-fetched, sir," added Sergeant Curtis as he saw the inspector look somewhat sceptical, "but after all, he very nearly got away with that too. The young man only just escaped being killed."

"Very true," said the inspector. "As a matter of fact I agree with you that the doctor is our man, and I'm inclined to agree that it happened just as you say. How to prove it, though, is quite another matter."

"We could get him on dangerous driving," said the sergeant doubtfully.

"Of course we couldn't," was the uncompromising reply. "His story is that Mr. Fenwick moved forward and then braked very suddenly. The sort of thing that is happening all the time, only fortunately not in quite such critical places. Our story would be that he deliberately drove into the back of Mr. Fenwick's little car so as to shunt it forward into the heavy traffic on the main road. Which of these two alternatives would you believe, if you were presented with them without any other facts? Be honest now."

The sergeant had to admit that his suggestion was not worth following up. "I think I'll have another talk with Mrs. Westbrook, if it's all the same to you, sir," he added. "She wasn't giving any information at all when I saw her before, but she may feel differently now she knows that Myrtle only left her five hundred pounds. It's downright insulting after she'd been expecting half the estate."

"It is indeed, and she may well feel vindictive. But wouldn't you expect it to be in the opposite direction? She'll be so mad at Myrtle for treating her so badly that she'll do all she can to protect the man who murdered him. However, go and see her by all means."

The sergeant was just about to leave when the telephone rang and the inspector motioned him to wait. "That was Jill Myrtle," he said later, replacing the receiver. "Says she has reason to suspect that it was Mrs. Westbrook who found Mr. Myrtle's dossier on the doctor. She also says that Mrs. Westbrook and the doctor seem to have had some sort of understanding for some time—'thick as thieves' was the phrase she used. Not very original."

The sergeant did not hear this last remark. "That's it!" he cried with as near an approach to excitement as he ever showed. "If Mrs. Westbrook found the dirt on the doctor she'd have a hold over him, wouldn't she? And if she told him she'd seen him put dope in the wine she'd have an even bigger hold over him. Now what use would she want to make of it?"

"Is he a rich man?"

"Very classy home, but I think he lives up to the hilt."

"That wouldn't stop her trying. Better not make it too plain that we're accusing her of blackmail—just a strong enough hint to scare her into giving herself away. Or giving him away. Yes, I think it really would be worth your while to pay her another visit."

But Sergeant Curtis was destined not to see Felicity Westbrook again, nor Dr. Jephcott either. Finding Felicity neither at the Old Manor nor at North Lane Cottage, the sergeant went straight to the modern Georgian house overlooking Southdene village green. A very angry-looking fashion-plate of a middle-aged lady and a very frightened-looking jodhpur-clad daughter came to the door. Dr. Ian Jephcott, it appeared, had done a bunk. And not alone. Mrs. Jephcott had no doubt at all who the new girl-friend was but she had no idea where they could have gone.

"We shall make enquiries immediately," promised the sergeant.

And some hours later he said to the inspector: "There you are, sir. It looks as if our hunch was right. The lady's been playing a double game. Hoping for Myrtle but keeping the doctor in reserve. Oh well, we shall find them in due course. It's all straightforward stuff now."

━━━16━━━

"They appear to have gone for sanctuary to one of those tax-haven islands," said Nevil. "Apparently Dr. Jephcott had been stacking cash away there from time to time. Against a demand from the Inland Revenue, I take it, and not for fear of a different kind of criminal prosecution."

The vicar and Clive and Angela were having a Sunday afternoon tea in the big sitting-room. March had come in with a burst of unusually mild and sunny weather, and the vicarage garden was glowing with yellow blossom.

"I wonder if they'll get away with it," said Clive.

"Nobody seems to know. The whole thing seems to be bogged down in one of those hopeless tangles of international law. I am very glad indeed that it is not my job to deal with it nor even to try to understand it. Does it worry you, Clive? Do you still feel revengeful for your mother's death?"

"I suppose it ought to, but I'm afraid it doesn't worry me so very much. Not now," said Clive. "Because if it hadn't been for Dr. Jephcott, you see, I might not be here. Not here in this very room, I mean. Jill's very envious of me. She's threatening to bribe you into adopting her by making an enormous donation to the roof fund."

"Well, that would be very generous of her," said the vicar, "but about your being here—both of you, that is. I'm afraid we're none of us going to be here for much longer."

"Dad!" Angela was indignant. "You've not gone and done it!"

"Well, yes, I'm afraid I have. No, don't interrupt. Give me a chance to tell you."

Nevil held up a hand as a furious tirade came from both Angela and Clive at once.

"I really do think it will be wise to make a change," he continued. "I've been here quite a long time and need a fresh challenge. Nobody is kicking me out, I assure you. It's entirely my own decision. I could ask for another parish. Or I could accept one of two offers of a very different kind that have been made to me. Both of them I find rather interesting. Would you like to hear?"

Clive and Angela indicated that they would.

"There is apparently to be one of those endless television serials," went on Nevil, "in which one of the main characters is a rather trendy person. Plenty of scope for showing what used to be called the seamy side of life, combined with a little bit of moral sentiment now and then. That's one offer."

Clive and Angela groaned.

"No, no. Don't be like that. I have to consider it very seriously," said Nevil.

"What's the other offer?" asked Angela.

"The other suggestion is a very much less lucrative one. In fact I doubt very much whether it would even mean as much as my present income, with no certainty from year to year that even that minimum would be maintained."

"Well, you don't have to worry about us any more," said Clive. "Angy and Ronnie can look after themselves, and after next week I shall be earning a pittance as a sort of glorified office boy in a publishing firm." He made a face. "Not to mention that Jill keeps trying to slip me enormous cheques."

"Buying your affection," said Angela. "She'll end by giving all the money away again in order to win your love. Don't you ever dare to desert her, Clive. Now, Dad. What's all this about? You've obviously decided on the second alternative and you're scared of telling me. I know the symptoms."

"There are so many of these little groups now, trying to help the greatest unfortunates in our society," said the vicar, "that you probably won't have heard of Refuge."

The others shook their heads.

"They are working mainly on run-down housing estates and in the derelict areas of inner cities," Nevil went on. "I think they probably overlap with some of the other associations but they seem to be meeting a need. At any rate, I like the look of the people who are running it and they seem to like the look of me."

"Where are you going to do this work?" asked Angela resignedly.

"London, to start with."

"And where are you going to live?"

"They've got a big Victorian house, as a home for people discharged from mental hospitals with nowhere to go. I shall start off there."

"But you won't be comfortable," protested Clive. "It won't be good for you."

"It can't be much colder than it is in this vicarage," retorted Nevil, "and it will be very good for me indeed. It will induce in me a certain humility, which is a virtue in which I am sadly lacking."

"That's very true," said Angela, "but you're not telling the whole truth, are you? You really want to leave the ministry of the Church, don't you? You've never believed in all its teaching. It's always been a bit of an act, hasn't it?"

Nevil got up and wandered over to the window before saying, with unwonted intensity: "Would you really like to know what I believe?"

"Yes, if it doesn't take too long," replied Angela.

"It can't take too long. I've got to get ready for evensong soon. We don't know very much, do we, we human creatures, for all our amazing discoveries and achievements. Right?"

"Right."

"But there are two things that we all know for sure. We know we must die and we know there is such a thing as love. Right?"

"Right."

"Well, I believe that God is love, and that love can conquer all things, even death. That's my creed. Very simple. Very trite."

And he left the room.

Clive looked at Angela and laughed. "You can't win," he said.

Anna Clarke was born in Cape Town and educated in Montreal and at Oxford. She holds degrees in both economics and English literature and has had a wide variety of jobs, mostly in publishing and university administration. She is the author of many previous suspense novels, including *One of Us Must Die*, *Letter from the Dead*, *Game Set and Danger*, and *Desire to Kill*.